'Feeling better this morning?'

'I'm fine, just fine,' Anna said.

'Good.' Dr Carroll picked up her wrist and took her pulse. Anna cursed as the stupid thing began to race. He'd think he was making her nervous! It really wasn't necessary to hold the patient's gaze quite so intently while taking a pulse.

'Why don't you get a car?' he demanded.

She resented the inquisition. 'I prefer riding a bicycle, and——'

'And it's environmentally sound,' he said, anticipating her words with a certain wryness, yet not real sarcasm. 'Very commendable, I'm sure, but not if you kill yourself in the process.'

Judith Worthy lives in an outer suburb of Melbourne, Australia, with her husband. When not writing, she can usually be found birdwatching, or gardening. She also likes to listen to music, and the radio, paints a little, likes to travel, and is concerned about conservation and animal cruelty. As well as romantic fiction, she also writes books for children.

Previous titles

CONDITION CRITICAL
DOCTOR DARLING

CROSSROADS OF THE HEART

BY

JUDITH WORTHY

MILLS & BOON LIMITED
ETON HOUSE   18–24 PARADISE ROAD
RICHMOND   SURREY   TW9 1SR

*First published in Great Britain 1992
by Mills & Boon Limited*

© Judith Worthy 1992

*Australian copyright 1992
Philippine copyright 1992
This edition 1992*

ISBN 0 263 77593 3

*Set in 10 on 12 pt Linotron Times
03-9203-52806
Typeset in Great Britain by Centracet, Cambridge
Made and printed in Great Britain*

CHAPTER ONE

'How *long* is a year?' Meg Lester rolled her eyes at the ceiling. 'Forever, in my reckoning, at least while *that* man is around!'

Used to her flatmate's tendency to exaggerate, Anna Mackay laughed. 'Come on, he can't be that bad! There isn't a man alive who could faze you, Meg.'

She switched off the hairdrier and ran her fingers testingly through her long brown hair. Newly washed, it gleamed in the firelight which was also reflected in her deep brown eyes, now glowing with a curiosity she couldn't deny.

Meg swallowed the last of her cocoa and brandished the mug. 'You wait! You'll find out, my girl. Dr Carroll will be the bane of your existence in next to no time, mark my words. And when you want my shoulder to cry on, don't say I didn't warn you.'

She reached out to fling another log on the fire. Sparks flew—as apparently they did between Meg and the new doctor at Mount William Hospital where they were both nurses, Anna mused wryly. She stretched her long legs towards the blaze. If everything Meg had told her was true, Dr Carroll had everyone he came in contact with shivering in their shoes.

'I can't wait to meet this medical monster!' she murmured. 'He's here for the whole year, you said?'

'The whole year,' echoed Meg gloomily. 'Twelve whole months, fifty-two weeks, three hundred and sixty-five days—no, three hundred and sixty-six, seeing it's Leap Year.' She groaned. 'It's a life sentence!'

'Not quite,' said Anna mischievously. 'You've already done three weeks.'

Dr Carroll had arrived the week after Anna had left on holiday, so she had not yet met the surgical registrar who had come to replace a very popular doctor who had gone overseas for a year. According to Meg, he demanded the ultimate in efficiency, had everyone running around in small circles to achieve it, and let them know in no uncertain terms when he wasn't satisfied. According to Meg, he had a very short fuse.

Anna took a lot of what her flatmate and nursing colleague said with a few grains of salt, but she did feel a tiny bit apprehensive. There must be something in what Meg said. . . She sighed. Life had always been so pleasant at Mount William, and she did not look forward to any disruption of that harmony. She had nothing against efficiency, but some people could be a bit overbearing.

'Anyway, let's forget Carroll,' said Meg. 'Tell me all about your trip. Did you meet any dishy men?'

'Hundreds,' drawled Anna, her smile teasing. 'But I wasn't in the mood. . .'

Meg threw a cushion at her. 'I bet Fiji was nice and warm, though.'

'Lovely! I could hardly bear to drag myself back to winter.'

Meg pushed up the sleeves of her outsize pink mohair sweater and leaned towards the fire. 'It's been arctic here—or should I say antarctic?' She laughed. 'You know, when I decided to come to Australia I expected it to be warm and sunny all the time, didn't you?'

Anna shook her head. 'Not really, not in this part of Victoria. Cam—my brother—had already lived here for a couple of years, so. . .so Mum and I had a fair idea what to expect.' She paused, annoyed at the sudden lump in her throat, the slipping of control.

Meg looked sympathetically across at her friend. 'It's OK, Anna, I understand. You're going to miss her pretty badly for a long while, I expect. And without the rest of your family. . .'

Anna stood up quickly. 'Let's have another mug of cocoa, shall we? And then I'd better get to bed or I'll never be up in the morning. Mustn't be late on my first morning back.'

She left Meg taking up the needles to continue knitting what looked like another outsize sweater in the fluffy kind of yarn she favoured, and went along the chill passageway to the kitchen. There was no central heating in the old weatherboard house they shared, so they spent most evenings at home in the living-room with the open fire lit. Anna shivered as she switched on the kettle and spooned cocoa into their mugs. Winter in the Central Highlands could be every bit as cold as home. It was no wonder Meg spent most of her spare time knitting warm sweaters.

Anna heaved another deep sigh. What was she going to do with her spare time now? She had felt restless and aimless somehow since her mother had died a couple of months ago. Moving in with Meg had helped, especially in the beginning, but the holiday which was supposed to be restorative had only made her feel more restive than ever.

She had even begun to think of going back to England, but she wasn't sure that was the solution. She'd been away three years and most of her friends were already married and scattered. She had few relatives. Her only close ones were her brother Cam and his wife and children, and they were in Canada now. She didn't want to go there. Not because Canada didn't attract her, but because she didn't want to be a hanger-on, a spinster aunt trailing around after her brother.

She hadn't really wanted to come to Australia, but after her first stroke her mother had yearned to be near her son and her grandchildren. Cam had written glowingly of Mount William, with its tree-lined streets and restored colonial buildings. It was a fast-growing tourist centre for the Grampians, and he had joined an expanding computer firm there. There was a shortage of nurses at the hospital, he'd told Anna, emphasising that it was expanding rapidly too and offered wide-ranging medical services.

Anna stared at her reflection in the uncovered kitchen window. She looked as though she was outside. And I am, she thought, I'm an outsider. I don't belong here or there or anywhere. I'm not even doing what I wanted to do.

The kettle boiled and she reached up and pulled the blind down over the window. Tears blinded her for a moment, but they were not so much tears of grief for her mother as the uncharacteristic bitterness which seemed to be pervading her lately. When her mother was still alive, needing her, Anna had felt her life had some purpose and she'd nursed no regrets, but lately she had begun to feel that life was passing her by. She was twenty-four, and the future seemed to have no tangible shape, nothing in it to look forward to.

'Don't be such a misery,' she muttered, shaking biscuits out of a packet on to a plate. 'Stop brooding

and pull yourself together. Something will turn up. . .'
She laughed softly, ironically, at her own optimism.
She clutched the two mugs of steaming cocoa in one
hand, the plate of biscuits in the other, and strode
resolutely back to the living-room. She mustn't let Meg
see her feelings too often. Meg was kind, but there was
nothing more she could do to help.

The next morning was fine, but icy. Meg was working
a middle shift, so Anna cycled to the hospital. The
house they rented was a couple of miles out of town,
and, although Meg had a car, Anna preferred to use a
bicycle herself, except in very bad weather when she
took the car if Meg didn't need it, or went with her if
Meg was leaving at the same time anyway.

Wrapped up in a thick sweater, her green parka and
the matching beret and gloves Meg had knitted her,
she kept her head down against the cold wind. Today
the road was a little treacherous, with black ice appear-
ing every now and then to catch the unwary, and twice
she nearly skidded into the verge. There were a few
other houses scattered along the road, some well set
back on smallholdings of only a few acres, but there
was no traffic at that early hour of the morning, with
the sun barely up. She did not in fact see a soul until
she came up to the nursery.

Mr Lattimer was unloading plants and gave her a
cheery wave and greeting. Anna paused for a few
moments.

'The holiday was great, thanks,' she said in answer
to his question. 'A bit warmer than it is here!'

The old man glanced at the sky with disgust. 'Don't
know what's going on up there,' he remarked darkly.
'Weather's not behaving the way it ought—cold when

it ought be warm, dry when it ought to be wet. Plants don't know when to flower and fruit. I reckon that greenhouse effect is on us already.'

'Could be,' Anna agreed.

'Normally I'm getting my tomatoes ready to go outside by now,' said the nurseryman, 'but this year. . .' He shook his head. 'This is a real cold snap, and goodness knows what's in front of us, what with that hole in the ozone.'

Yes, thought Anna with a sudden sinking of spirits again, who knows what's in front of us?

'Well, I'd better be going,' she said. 'Mustn't be late on my first morning back at work.'

'Here,' said Mr Lattimer abruptly, and shoved a pot-plant at her, 'cheer the place up a bit with a few flowers. These'll last longer than a vase of cut blooms.'

While she thanked him, he stowed the largish terra-cotta pot of freesias in her handlebars basket. He often gave her a bunch of flowers, and despite her frequent protests would never let her pay for them. He'd been her patient once, needing careful nursing after a car accident, and he insisted it was due to her he'd been able to go back to work. Anna's insistence that she was only one of a team did not move him at all, so she accepted his floral expressions of gratitude graciously.

She cycled on with the heavy perfume from her gift wafting back in her face. She smiled a little as she recalled Meg's warning as she'd gone off to bed last night.

'Don't forget, watch out for Dr Carroll!'

I will, Anna thought, you bet I will! She was just as intrigued this morning at the thought of this ogre as she had been last night, and was trying to picture him from Meg's scathing description. She slowed at the crossroads where she had to turn right and head for town, and noticed a car in the distance, but it was far enough away to give her plenty of time to negotiate the junction. That was, if it hadn't been for the ice.

Right in the middle of the intersection she went into a skid on an unseen patch of black ice that demanded all her skill to keep the bicycle under control. As she slewed wildly across the treacherous road surface, she caught her breath, certain she was going to fall off, and at the same time was deafened by the screeching of brakes as the car loomed up beside her and she went flying through the air accompanied by the pot of freesias, while the bicycle careered off on its own, as did her beret.

'Stupid bloody wench!'

A couple of seconds later Anna, spreadeagled on the grassy verge, looked up into angry grey eyes which immediately swam before her. Something cool and soft lay on her cheek, and as she tried to lift a hand to brush it off another hand, large with warm fingertips, intervened. Anna glimpsed a crushed freesia bloom in his fingers, moaned softly and passed out.

When she came to she was still lying on the ground, but there was a blanket over her, and she was lying on another. She seemed to be quite alone. She lifted her head gingerly, found that it hurt and she felt nauseous, so sank back again. She had glimpsed the car parked a few yards away, but there was no sign of the occupant, the owner of the grey eyes, the man who had called her. . . Anna's skin prickled in indignation. Anybody could fall foul of black ice, and he must have been travelling too fast, especially coming up to a cross-roads. . . She tried again to get up.

'Don't move!'

The command was a whipcrack on the cold air, the steely Australian male voice so authoritative that she obeyed. He must have been in the car and the angle of it had concealed him from her. Now he was standing over her.

'How are you feeling?' He squatted beside her, and eye contact with him made her feel dizzy again.

'I'm all right. . .' she protested, preparing to throw the blanket off, but she was thwarted by strong arms which insisted she lie prone.

'You've done one stupid thing today, don't compound it with another,' the motorist said scathingly. 'You might have injured your spine. I've rung for an ambulance on the car-phone. It should be here soon.'

'The ice,' she said. 'I skidded on black ice. . .'

'You came out of that side-road without looking right or left,' he accused.

'I did! But anyway, there's never any traffic at this time of the morning.' Indignation made her add, 'You're supposed to slow down at crossroads.'

He was standing over her again, a tall, intimidating figure, with broad shoulders silhouetted against the sky, his features rugged like the mountains behind him, dark brown wavy hair lifting in the slight breeze, and with a kind of wild and lonely look about him, Anna thought, then wiped the thought. Was she delirious? He was a rude, abrasive individual, not some romantic Heathcliff figure, for heaven's sake! But he was concerned about her. . . No, he was just doing the right thing while regarding her as a nuisance, and a stupid wench at that!

'I'm sorry,' she said. Then, 'Look, I'm sure there's nothing wrong with me. I feel fine.' She raised her head again, and this time a shaft of pain shot through it and she fell back. He knelt beside her quickly and she felt warm fingers clasp her wrist. Her pulse beat raggedly against his touch.

'Concussion,' he said, his voice not quite so abrasive. 'I suspect you were hit by the flowerpot. You were all over freesias, and you've still got potting mix on your face.'

The ludicrousness of it had evidently not struck him, but Anna felt a smile starting. 'My poor freesias,' she muttered, and then a possibility occurred to her. 'Are you a doctor?'

He nodded. 'Now, don't move any more. I don't think there are any bones broken, but it's better to be sure than sorry. We'll get you to the hospital and X-rayed and then we'll know. So just lie quiet, there's a good girl.'

I don't know him, Anna thought fuzzily, her brain not working as sharply as usual. He's not one of the town GPs. . .

Her thoughts were cut short by the arrival of the ambulance. In her absence there had obviously been changes, and she did not recognise the two young paramedics who eased her gently on to a stretcher and carried her into the ambulance, but to her surprise they knew the motorist.

'How'd it happen, Dr Carroll?' one young man asked.

Anna's brain absorbed his name with a jolt that made her blood pound. Dr Carroll! Surely not. . .oh, no, it couldn't be, but it must be. . . And her first encounter with him had to be like this! She squirmed under her blanket and did not, as she had intended, tell the ambulance men she was a nurse at the hospital. She could just imagine the kind of look she'd get from

Dr Carroll. It was going to be bad enough when he did find out.

'My bike—what about my bike?' she managed to say as a sudden anxiety over it pushed other thoughts aside.

'I'll see to it,' Dr Carroll said brusquely, and the next moment the ambulance doors were shut tight and she was on her way to the hospital.

Meg was right, she thought, he isn't exactly charming. Stupid wench indeed! The recollection made her flush with indignation all over again. She gritted her teeth and clenched her fists. If Meg was only half right about him, and Anna was willing to believe now that she was, Dr Carroll was never going to let her forget this incident. He didn't have even a glimmer of a sense of humour. What a way to start!

The ambulance was at the hospital within minutes and Anna was swiftly transferred from it to the casualty department. 'Good grief!' exclaimed the sister in charge, Cheryl Walker. 'It's you! This is a funny way to return from holidays! What happened?'

'I got knocked down by a car,' Anna groaned. 'There was black ice on the road and I skidded.'

'Riding your bike, I suppose,' said Cheryl. 'Daft thing to do in this weather.' She was another Pom, from Cheshire.

'More than daft—downright dangerous.' The iron-clad voice was Dr Carroll's. 'She's lucky to be alive—careering all over the road and not looking where she was going. I could have killed her!'

'Oh, hello, Dr Carroll.' Cheryl's voice took on a slight edge and she directed a meaningful glance at Anna. Then what he had said sank in. 'It was you who knocked Anna down?' She was aghast.

He was standing there so rigidly, Anna thought, as to be almost inanimate.

He said, 'Unfortunately, yes. I don't think there's much damage, slight concussion maybe, but we'll soon see.'

Anna writhed under his gaze, hardly daring to meet those flinty grey eyes that raked her face and shrank her self-assurance to nil.

'Poor old Anna,' clucked Cheryl sympathetically. 'Imagine arriving as a casualty on your first day back at work!' Her eyes sparkled with amusement. At least she could see the funny side of it. 'If you're going to be out of action, Simone'll have to manage your ward for a bit longer, I suppose.'

Anna swallowed. The cat was out of the bag now.

Dr Carroll was not slow. As though Anna wasn't capable of answering for herself, he said, 'She works here?'

Cheryl's eyebrows lifted. 'Oh, didn't she tell you? Sister Mackay is in charge of Women's Surgical. She's just back from holidays today. What a thing to happen——' Her explanation broke off as he snapped an impatient look at her.

Then he considered Anna for a long moment, before saying, 'I see.'

Anna knew she was damned. His eyes said it. He was going to give her hell, worse hell than maybe he ordinarily would have done, because he'd reckon she'd earned it. Stupid bloody wench, that was what he thought of her.

And the torment was starting right now. If she'd hoped to escape seeing Dr Carroll again, she had of course hoped in vain. If she'd hoped he would leave her treatment to someone else, she had again hoped in vain. Evidently he was anxious to make sure personally that his victim was not badly hurt. No doubt worried about his insurance, Anna thought grimly, as she was wheeled away to have her spine X-rayed and steeled herself to undergo the ministrations of the redoubtable Dr Carroll. There was just one thing Meg had not mentioned about him—that he was rivetingly hand-some, that even when he was angry, as he certainly was with Anna, his deep-set grey eyes had a spine-tingling effect that was more than a little disconcerting.

CHAPTER TWO

ANNA felt a fool. And a fraud. She had a few grazes
and a couple of bruises that were going to develop in
Technicolor, but the X-rays had shown no fractures or
internal injuries. She had been lucky to fall on springy
grass in soft earth, and the flowerpot had merely grazed
her temple. But Dr Carroll had insisted she be put to
bed and kept in overnight for observation. He made
no bones about her good luck.

'Thank your lucky stars you fell where you did,' he
said when he had thoroughly examined her for external
injuries, an examination which for some reason embarrassed her. 'And the flowerpot didn't catch you more
than a glancing blow.'

Relieved, Anna couldn't help grinning. 'Wait till I
tell Mr Lattimer!'

'Who is?' he queried, drawing the sheet up over her,
and leaving her skin still tingling, even from the purely
clinical touch of his hands.

'Lattimer's Nursery. Maybe you don't know it. Mr
Lattimer often gives me flowers. Today it was a pot-
plant. . .well, bulbs. . . Oh, what a shame they were
ruined. . .' She wavered as Cheryl had done under his
solid stare. His eyebrows were thick and dark, almost
meeting. His mouth was firm, set in deep creases, and
belonged, Anna thought, to someone who didn't waste
words.

He had left her abruptly once satisfied she was all in
one piece—and not likely to sue him for negligence,

Anna decided wryly—and she had meekly submitted
to the ministrations of her colleagues for the first time
in her life. They had taken her to a small unoccupied
ward and fussed over her—unnecessarily, she protested, but as reaction to the accident set in she felt
suddenly fragile and was comforted by all the attention.

Aided by a sedative, she slept for some hours. When
she woke she was at first at a loss, then, recognising
her surroundings, she tried to get out of bed, but a
weakness seemed to have gripped her and she fell back
against the pillows. As she remembered the events of
the morning, she covered her face with her hands in
dismay.

Presently Meg came in, all sunny smiles and jocular.
'Well, well, get you!' she ribbed. 'Imagine being run
over by Carroll himself! He must have been livid. Your
life won't be worth living now.' She laughed at the face
Anna pulled, and perched on the end of the bed.
'Actually the whip hand might be yours—every time
he gets nasty you could threaten to sue.'

'How could I? I'm not hurt,' Anna protested weakly.
Suing someone was not something she would want to
do anyway.

'Well, your bike's a write-off.'

'How do you know?'

'The police brought it round to the house just before
lunch. It'd cost more to repair than buying a new one,
they said. You ought to get him to pay.'

'I think he might—argue the toss,' Anna said,
shrinking from even tackling Dr Carroll over it. 'He
said it was my fault.'

'Was it?'

'Well, I suppose it was, partly. He said I wasn't
looking, but I did, both ways, before I started across

the intersection. I'd seen the car in the distance, but it must have come up pretty fast, and when I skidded on the ice. . .' Anna shrugged. 'It all happened so quickly. I'm just glad it wasn't worse.'

'Sounds as though he was to blame, if you ask me,' said Meg with some satisfaction. 'Of course that'll make him even tetchier. He'd hate being in the wrong.' She glanced at the bedside table. 'Say, who brought you flowers?'

'Flowers?' Anna hadn't noticed. 'No one's been but you. . . Well, I suppose while I was asleep someone might have. . . I don't know, Meg.' Her eyes focused on the tumbler full of pale cream flowers and for the first time she was aware of their distinctive perfume. 'Freesias,' she murmured, and the astonishing thought entered her mind that Dr Carroll might have brought them. Don't be daft, she chided herself. Why on earth would he do that?

'Maybe you have a secret admirer,' said Meg. She glanced at her watch. 'I'd better go. I promised Valda I'd only be fifteen minutes—we've got every bed occupied. Thank goodness the football season's almost over! What those local yokels do to their knees, elbows and collarbones defies description.' She rose and looked anxiously at Anna. 'Sure you're all right?'

'Positive. It's a lot of fuss about nothing.'

Meg gave her hand a squeeze. 'You know, when I saw your mangled bike and there was no you, I nearly flipped. Don't take any chances, Anna. Stay here till Carroll says you can go. Concussion's not funny, you know.'

When she'd gone, Anna stared for a few moments at the freesias. It was just a coincidence, of course.

Freesias were common as weeds at the moment. One of the nurses must have put them there.

A few minutes later a nurse came in to check on her. It was one of her friends, Sally Hunter. Anna accepted her teasing in good grace, realising that her spill was going to provoke more than a few jokes at her expense until some other event eclipsed it.

Sally plumped pillows and straightened covers and asked if she wanted anything to eat. Anna wasn't hungry. She said she'd wait until teatime.

'I dare say Dr Carroll will be round to see you later,' Sally said. 'He popped in earlier, but you were still asleep. Quite a few people have been asking after you.'

'Who brought the flowers?' Anna asked casually.

Sally shook her head. 'Don't know. Probably one of the other nurses—we had lots over today.' She turned as she went out. 'Use your bell if you want anything. Just because you're staff it doesn't mean you can't have service!'

'Thanks!' Anna felt very peculiar being a patient. It was the first time ever, she realised.

A few more of her colleagues dropped in over the next little while, but there was no sign of Dr Carroll, and eventually she slept.

She woke next morning feeling much better and ready to go home—or to start work. It really was a fuss over nothing, she thought crossly when the nurse in charge insisted she wait until Dr Carroll had said she could be discharged.

'It'd be more than life was worth to let you go without permission,' she said. 'He'll be round shortly.'

So Anna waited impatiently, and finally her door opened and he came in. She had been ready to take him to task, to demand that he discharge her at once, but all her fire seemed to evaporate when he appeared. He crossed to the bed, looking more formidable than ever in a white coat.

'Feeling better this morning?' he greeted her tersely, but kindly enough.

'I'm fine, just fine,' Anna said.

He looked down at her. 'Headache?'

'No.'

'Dizzy?'

'Not now.'

'Good.' He picked up her wrist and took her pulse. Anna cursed as the stupid thing began to race. He'd think he was making her nervous! It really wasn't necessary to hold the patient's gaze quite so intently while taking a pulse.

He dropped her hand back on the coverlet. 'Well, I think you can go home now. But take care. With concussion you can get delayed reactions even after a few days. Any sign of a headache, dizziness, nausea, any other unusual symptoms, report it at once. OK?'

'Of course,' said Anna, through gritted teeth. She did, after all, know the symptoms of concussion.

He was still looking steadily at her. 'My insurance will replace your bicycle. You should have a new one delivered in a few days. The shop will phone you.'

Anna was speechless. 'That's—that's very——'

He brushed aside her attempt to thank him. 'I don't accept that I was in any way to blame, but I've given you the benefit of the doubt so far as the insurance is concerned. I dare say you didn't have the bike insured?'

'No. . .'

'I would suggest that you don't attempt to ride for a

week at least,' he went on, 'and then not on days when there's likely to be ice on the roads.'

'I haven't got any other means of transport,' Anna protested. 'Except when Meg doesn't want her car.'

'Why don't *you* get a car?' he demanded.

She resented the inquisition. 'I prefer riding a bicycle. It's good exercise, for one thing, and——'

'And environmentally sound,' he said, anticipating her words with a certain wryness, yet not real sarcasm. 'Very commendable, I'm sure, but not if you kill yourself in the process.'

'I'll be much more careful in future,' Anna said, astonished at her own meekness. She adopted a brisker tone. 'Good. Well, if I can go now. . . I might as well start work. I bet they're short-staffed as usual on my ward——'

'Not until tomorrow,' he interrupted. 'And then only if you haven't developed any worrying symptoms in the meantime. I suggest you take it easy for the rest of today. Your friend Sister Lester will be here shortly to take you home, and I'll pick you up in the morning.'

'But. . .' Anna was completely bowled over again.

'I don't know how else you intend to get to work,' he said, 'while Sister Lester needs her car to get here later in the day, unless you intend to wake her up early or arrange for someone else to give you a lift. Since I live more or less in your direction, it might as well be me.'

His logic was faultless. She couldn't expect Meg, who didn't get home until midnight, to get up at dawn just to drive her to work. 'You seem to have worked it all out,' she said resignedly.

'Which is more than you seem to have done,' he commented.

Anna accepted the rebuke. 'It just seems a bit of a cheek to expect you to. . .'

His grey eyes were steady, penetrating. 'I do have some sense of responsibility,' he said, 'even if I wasn't to blame. And your place is only a couple of miles out of my way.'

Arrogant! she thought, prickling with annoyance again. Condescending too. He didn't want her to think he was putting himself out for her. Then she softened a little. He could easily have been a lot less concerned about her.

'Well, I'm grateful,' she said. 'Thank you.' At least it was only a short distance from Meg's house to town, so she wouldn't have to suffer the nervous tension of riding with him for long. And it was only until she got her new bike.

Meg was all agog when she drove Anna home. 'You've really turned him on his ear,' she crowed. 'Serve the so-and-so right!'

'No doubt he'll have his revenge,' Anna commented gloomily. 'I dare say I'll be required to pay for it.' She glanced at the bunch of freesias tucked into her bag, wondering why she had bothered to bring them home.

'Poor you!' said Meg, with a grimace. She added, grudgingly, 'I must say he sounded quite nice when he rang up and asked if I could come and fetch you home. It seems he does have his moments!' She gave Anna a speculative look. 'You'd better watch out in more ways than one!'

Anna treated that remark with the contempt she thought it deserved, and Meg laughed.

It was just after Meg had left for the hospital that afternoon that there was a knock at the door. Anna found Ned Lattimer on the doorstep with a big bunch of flowers and a pot of primroses.

'Seeing the freesias brought you bad luck,' he said with a grin, 'I thought maybe you'd rather have primroses. They're the real thing, Sister, genuine English primroses.'

He thrust the pot of delicate pale creamy blooms into her hands, and Anna almost wept at his goodheartedness.

'Ned, I can see they are. Oh, how lovely! But you shouldn't have. . .'

'Thought they might cheer you up,' he said. 'Coming off your bike like that must have churned you up a bit.'

'How did you know?' asked Anna.

'That doctor friend of yours told me when he came in for the freesias. He seemed real upset that the pot was smashed and the flowers crushed. I told him no worries, I'd replace it, but he still insisted on taking a bunch of blooms and paying for them.' He grinned. 'Reckon he might have a bit of a shine on you, Sister.'

Anna was startled and astonished. 'Oh, no—no, definitely not, Ned. He was the one who knocked me down. . .'

'Yeah, so he said. Churned him up no end too, I reckon.'

She laughed awkwardly. 'Well, I assure you there was no personal reason for the flowers. He just felt— er—responsible for my losing the first lot.'

Ned was backing off the veranda. 'Well, got to finish my deliveries. Be seeing you. Take care, won't you?'

'Thank you! Ned, thank you so much,' Anna called after him, quite overcome with his gift, and what he had revealed. Did Dr Carroll have a soft spot under all that armour plating after all, or was it just a strong sense of duty?

Anna waited in some trepidation for Dr Carroll to call for her the next morning. She half hoped he would have forgotten and she would have to ring for a taxi, but on the dot of seven he was tooting his horn. She was on at seven-thirty. He evidently wasn't going to be the cause of her being late.

Meg had come home last night dead tired and was still fast asleep, so Anna let herself quietly out of the house and ran down the path to the waiting car.

'Good morning,' she said brightly, getting in beside him.

'Morning,' he replied, and Anna guessed his clipped greeting was a signal that he did not want chirpy conversation from her. Well, that was fine so far as she was concerned.

'Feeling OK?' he asked in a rather depersonalised way.

'Yes, thanks.'

He glanced at the dressing on her temple. 'Watch that graze. Don't let it get infected.'

'No. . .'

'You'll have to keep off the wards if you do.'

'Of course.' So his remark wasn't concern for her, but for hospital hygiene.

As they passed Lattimer's Nursery, Anna couldn't help saying, 'Ned brought me some flowers yesterday and a new pot-plant. Primroses. . .' It was poking out of her bag, but Dr Carroll didn't even glance at it, or comment. She wanted to thank him for the freesias but wasn't sure how to. Would he have expected her to guess? And surely he must realise that Ned would mention his having been to the nursery. But what should she say. . .?

Finally, as they reached the crossroads and he stopped, she blurted out, 'Thank you for the freesias.'

For a moment she thought she'd put her foot in it, then something almost like a smile flickered fleetingly across his lips and he seemed momentarily embarrassed.

'I did wonder. . .' she ventured. 'But Ned mentioned you'd been there. It was a nice thought, but you didn't have to. . .'

He looked as though he did not appreciate being accused of harbouring nice thoughts, and then all at once his face relaxed. He said, deadpan, 'The insurance company wouldn't run to replacement flowers, I'm afraid.'

Heavens, he has got a sense of humour, Anna thought, relieved, but he chooses to keep it well hidden. The discovery pleased her. 'Well, thank you anyway,' she said, and, sensing he was impatient with gratitude, fell silent again for want of something else to say.

The mountains were a deep blue backdrop to the town, and she let her eyes drift across the scene, trying to concentrate on the picturesque features of the landscape in order to neutralise the tension she felt being next to the somewhat enigmatic Dr Carroll.

Suddenly he spoke. 'You're English? Where from?'

'Sussex. Ever been to Bognor?'

There was a flicker of interest in his sideways glance. 'A few years ago I think I went just about everywhere. How long are you here for?'

'If you mean in Australia, I emigrated three years ago. If you mean Mount William, I don't know—I might move on soon. . .' Anna stopped. What had possessed her to confide that when she hadn't even expressed her feelings to Meg, and she didn't particularly want the hospital to know yet that she was restless? She went on hastily, 'You're just here for a year while Russ Phillips is away, I take it.'

'If I can stick it that long,' he said.

Anna's eyebrows rose. 'What's the problem? Is Mount William Hospital not to your taste? Or is it the town?'

He took the car just a shade too fast across the bridge over the river that skirted the town. He was a good driver, she judged, with good reflexes, but perhaps a shade impatient.

'I'm not a country boy,' he confessed.

'Then why did you take this job?'

They were in the main street and heading up the hill to the hospital. Dr Carroll glanced at her, or, she thought, glared. 'Personal reasons.' He was curt as though her question had been intrusive.

However, she hardly heard his answer. She was suddenly sure he hadn't noticed the traffic lights ahead. They were, she was afraid, going to go through a red light. Unable to hold back, she exclaimed, 'Stop! It's on red!'

The car slammed to a halt, jerking her briefly against the restraining seat-belt.

'I can see that,' Dr Carroll said calmly, and Anna felt a fool, a silly panicky fool. Maybe he always screamed up to traffic lights like that. He turned to look at her. 'You are edgy. Maybe you should have taken another day off.'

'No, I'm fine. . .' But she was shaking inside.

She was glad when he swung the car into the doctors'

car park and she parted company with him. Perhaps the start to her day hadn't been as calamitous as yesterday, but it had left her feeling decidedly nerve-racked. Dr Carroll was certainly a puzzling man. For a few minutes in the car he'd been almost conversational, but then had seemed to regret the lapse. Anna shrugged as she went up to her ward. She had neither the time nor the inclination to try and analyse the man. Just let him keep out of her hair while she was on duty, that was all.

Simone Rosario was relieved to see Anna back. 'It's been hectic,' she admitted. 'And keeping one jump ahead of Doc Carroll requires mental agility of Olympic standard!'

'He seems to have acquired quite a reputation,' Anna commented.

'He keeps everybody on their toes,' Simone said. 'And woe betide you if you do something he doesn't like.' She inclined her head smilingly. 'But to give him his due, he's a first-rate medico, and the patients love him. Funny, isn't it, how a man can be a right pain to staff and practically Father Christmas to the patients?' She nodded slowly. 'He's a perfectionist, that's the trouble. He expects the same high standards he sets himself from others, and he's aggravated by lapses.'

'In medicine that's surely a commendable attitude,' Anna said. 'But I know what you mean—it can be damned hard to live up to that sort of expectation.' She smiled. 'I gather you don't altogether share the general awe of him, or wish him further away.'

Simone's face turned faintly pink. 'If you must know, I think he's probably a pretty wonderful person if you could only get to know him. But I've got a snowflake's chance in hell of ever doing that. I'm just another robot to him.'

'Does everyone always call him Dr Carroll?' Anna enquired, since she had become used to the casual practice of using first names even among the medical staff, at least off the wards.

'His name's Scott,' Simone told her. 'But I've never heard anyone except the other doctors use it.' She waved a sheaf of notes and went through the office door. 'Come on, I'd better fill you in on who's what. We're pretty full at the moment—all new patients too. And a range of medical conditions such as you never did see! Doc Carroll will be round at ten, and I expect he'll want you to shadow him today. I'll get the paperwork up to date and keep an eye on the others, if you like.' She pushed open one of the ward doors, and whispered, 'We've a new junior who keeps dropping things and losing things and getting in a tizz, but when she gets over her nerves she'll be good. That's her over there, bed-making with Fran. Liz Farmer's her name.'

Anna was introduced to Liz, who smiled broadly, answered Anna's casual questions about how she was enjoying her job, and then as she turned round to continue making the bed, tripped over the end of a blanket and fell flat on her face.

'Oh, Liz. . .!' exclaimed Simone, and burst out laughing, as did Fran and the four patients in the ward. Anna couldn't help smiling too, especially as Simone had just been telling her that Liz was accident-prone. Liz herself seemed to be convulsed with either laughter or tears, and Anna suspected it might be tears she was trying to disguise.

'May I ask what the joke is?'

At the sound of the deep male voice, Anna and the

other two nurses wheeled round. Dr Carroll's grim countenance showed no sign of amusement. The grey eyes lasered straight at Liz.

'What's that girl doing on the floor?' he demanded, pointing an accusing finger at the unfortunate Liz, who had been about to get to her feet, but who now froze, half prone.

Simone and Fran were both looking at Anna, who swallowed hard, realising that now she was back and in charge, she was expected to answer.

Calmly she faced the registrar. 'She tripped over,' she said in smooth tones.

'Is that something to cause everyone else to fall about laughing?' he rapped out.

'The way it happened was rather comical,' Anna explained, not letting his piercing gaze intimidate her. If there was going to be a harmonious working relationship between them, it was going to be out of mutual respect, not as a result of her being browbeaten.

His eyebrows surged together. He looked at Liz, who seemed to be cowering on the floor. 'Get up, girl! And get on with whatever you were doing. This is a hospital, not an entertainment centre. There are sick people here requiring your attention. I suggest you keep your mind on the job you came here to do, if you want to keep it.' He switched his gaze back to Anna, who, though seething inwardly, nevertheless said in cool tones,

'What can I do for you, Dr Carroll? I wasn't expecting you to come on rounds for another hour or so.'

She was aware of Liz, wide-eyed and white-faced, scrambling up off the floor to help Fran finish off the bed in utter silence, while Simone quietly melted away, and the patients all seemed suddenly to have retreated behind their books and magazines or had put their earphones on. It was almost as though a screen had been discreetly swung around her and Dr Carroll. He was her problem now!

'I want to talk to you,' he said peremptorily. 'In your office.'

Anna smiled. 'Of course.' She led the way out of the ward and marched briskly along to the charge sister's office. As he closed the door behind him, she said, 'Please sit down.' She remained standing herself.

He ignored the chair and perched on the edge of her desk. He did not speak immediately, but seemed more interested in examining her features. Suspecting that it was his method of intimidating lesser mortals, Anna steeled herself to make the opening remark.

'I haven't had time yet to review all the patients in my ward,' she said. 'Sister Rosario was about to take me round.'

His reply was the last thing Anna expected. 'Did you enjoy your holiday?'

'Yes, thank you,' she replied warily. 'I went to Fiji. It was warm and tranquil and I had a nice lazy time.'

'Well, I hope I shall be glad you're back.' Dr Carroll's grey eyes threw out a steely challenge. 'I trust it isn't normally as chaotic around here as it's been these past three weeks.'

Anna stiffened defensively. 'Chaotic? I don't know what you mean, Dr Carroll. Sister Rosario is very efficient.'

His mouth quirked a little. 'Perhaps we have different definitions of efficient, Sister.'

'Simone's workload was greatly increased while I was away,' Anna pointed out, and forced a smile to cover her real feelings.

He was not impressed. He stood up. 'Well, as I'm here, I might as well see the patients.'

Anna's glance flicked to the clock on the wall. 'It's a little early. Staff probably haven't finished giving medications yet.'

He was unperturbed. 'Since the majority of your patients require little more than a social call from me today, I don't think that will be a problem.' He gave her a flat kind of smile. 'I've noticed a little sloppiness in this ward which you might tighten up.'

Again she went rigid. 'Sloppiness? I should like you to explain.'

'For instance, a tendency for nurses to be gossiping and giggling when they should be concentrating on laying up the medications trolley accurately,' he said.

'I'm sure no mistakes have been made,' said Anna, fingers crossed.

'Maybe not, but the potential is there. They aren't filing clerks in an office where it doesn't matter if a letter is misfiled. If a mistake happens here it could be a matter of life and death.'

'You don't need to tell me that,' Anna said coldly, growing more and more incensed. What he was saying was perfectly right, but he didn't have to be so high and mighty about it. He might have grounds for criticism, but his manner of conveying it was not the kind to win friends and influence people.

There was a light tap at the door and Anna called, 'Come in!' hoping it might be someone to take this irritating man away from her for a while at least. Her good humour was fast evaporating and she was finding it difficult to control her temper.

But it was only Simone, who glanced briefly, and to Anna's eyes anxiously, from one to the other, before she handed Anna the sheaf of patients' notes and mumbled something about her needing them and that the examination trolley was laid up. Anna silently applauded Simone's forethought. She had anticipated that Dr Carroll might want to do his round right away.

'Thank you, Simone,' she said. 'Dr Carroll is going to do his round now, so if Fran isn't busy perhaps she could accompany us.'

Simone vanished and Dr Carroll strode to the door after her, clearly expecting Anna to follow, which she did. Later, she thought, she would try and work out tactics to cope with him. He wasn't the first incorrigible fault-finder she'd ever encountered.

Although she was annoyed with him at the moment, she was also intrigued. She was sure that matters were not quite what they seemed. Her judgement of people had always been pretty good, and there was definitely something bugging this man, she decided. Instinct told her that although he might be a perfectionist his impatience and irritability were probably exacerbated by something else, maybe something quite extraneous, and deep-rooted. She smiled at herself. Psychoanalysing everyone was one of her faults, but it sometimes did prove helpful.

Head held high, she sailed past Dr Carroll into the corridor as he held the door open. At least he had some manners, she thought grimly. The notes Simone had given her were in room order, so Anna headed straight back to the first ward, where the registrar had found her.

Fran and Liz had gone and the newly made bed sat innocently by the window waiting for the next admission. Their entrance was regarded with interest by the women in the ward. Anna smiled all round to convey

that all was well and there was no dissension, and Dr
Carroll stopped at the bed nearest the door.

'Good morning, Mrs Waite,' he greeted the stout
woman in it. 'How are you today?'

Good, thought Anna, he isn't one of those who say
'we'. She gave him a point, and drew the screens
around the bed. She glanced at the patient's notes
while he was making small talk and they waited for the
examination trolley. His bedside manner was friendly,
casual, without a trace of irritation or grumpiness, she
noted. Whatever was bugging him, it wasn't patients.
He had all the time in the world for them. Maybe he
just had it in for nurses. Unrequited love, jilted by a
nurse. . .her mind searched for reasons as her eyes
scanned the patient record. Mrs Waite had been admitted for treatment of varicose ulcers on her left leg.

Suddenly the registrar's voice penetrated Anna's
concentration. 'Where's that trolley?' he demanded in
an impatient aside. 'I need to examine this woman's
leg.'

Anna swallowed hard, but didn't have to pray,
because at that moment Fran came in breathlessly with
the trolley. She looked rattled already and dropped the
first packet of sterile gloves on the floor as she opened
them. Dr Carroll looked daggers at her and Anna
quickly opened another pack. He gave her an 'I told
you so' kind of look which she returned unruffled, even
though he was getting to her again.

The examination proceeded swiftly, and Anna was
impressed with Dr Carroll's gentle handling of the limb,
the way consideration for the patient dictated his every
move. He replaced the bandage himself, then said, 'I
think we'll keep you in for a few more days, Mrs Waite.
The healing process is coming along nicely, but it'll be a

while yet before we can operate.' He turned to Anna. 'Make sure she sees the physio for massage to soften the indurated area around the edge of the ulcer, and keeps up her exercises.' He smiled at the patient. 'That's most important, Mrs Waite—exercise.'

As they moved away, leaving Fran to draw back the screens and follow, Dr Carroll said, 'Let me have her diabetes progress chart later, will you? I suspect she's not as stable as we'd like. We'll have to get her to lose some more weight. You might tell her GP I'd like a word with him too.'

'Yes, Doctor,' said Anna, and caught his eye. For a moment she thought that he thought she was mocking, but then to her amazement a glimmer of something like humour appeared in the grey irises, as it had when she'd thanked him for the freesias, and his upper lip twitched as though repressing an involuntary smile. He's human, she decided, with something like relief, and this helped her to get through what otherwise might have been a traumatic experience.

He didn't spare her, giving voice to criticisms often, and showing his impatience both with her and Fran, especially when an item was missing from the trolley and he had to wait while Fran fetched the required spatula. At the end, Anna was exhausted, but she had made a mental note to be a perfectionist too. She'd give him no grounds for complaint at all if she could help it.

As they returned to her office, she said briskly, 'I'll have someone bring you Mrs Waite's insulin chart, Mrs Grey's X-rays and the pathology report for Miss Gregory right away.'

Grey eyes roved over her face. Were they just a little softer, she wondered, or was that imagination? And what was that strange tingling sensation down her spine? A symptom that had better be imagination too, she thought, alarmed.

'And Mrs Gardiner's case history,' he reminded her sharply. 'You forgot her—the patient with gallstones, admitted two days ago. Of course, you weren't here then, were you? You were falling off bicycles and trying to get yourself killed.' Without waiting for a reply, he marched off in the direction of his office.

Chagrined at her omission, minor though it was, Anna drew her lips together tightly, wanting to spit. Imagination, *definitely*, she thought, on both counts.

CHAPTER THREE

'WELL, how was it? Did he eat you alive?' Meg came in on a draught of chill night air, flung her bag on the couch and herself after it.

'He tried,' said Anna, 'but didn't care for the taste! Spat me out in a kidney bowl.'

Meg laughed, absently picked up her knitting and carried on with it as though she'd been knitting all evening. 'I was dying to come and see how you were surviving,' she said, 'but it was hell on my ward today. Just as well Carroll didn't show up, or I might have resigned on the spot.' She looked sharply at Anna. 'Well, was I right or not?'

'You were right,' admitted Anna. 'He is scratchy, pernickety and all that, but——'

'Oh, come on, Anna, you're not going to make excuses for him!' Meg protested.

Anna put down the book she was reading and yawned. 'I hadn't realised it was so late until you came in. I'd better get to bed.'

'He's picking you up again tomorrow?'

'So he said—although, come to think of it, he didn't mention the fact today. I hope he doesn't forget.'

'He won't! He's Mr Perfection himself, remember.'

Anna shook her head. 'He's as human as everyone else, Meg, and probably fallible too. For instance, he must have been speeding to have knocked me off my bike.'

'You call that fallibility?' said Meg, disgusted. 'I call it arrogance.'

Anna gazed for a moment into the dying embers of the fire. 'No, I'm sure he's angry with himself about it, and I'm also sure he sets as stringent standards for himself as anyone else and punishes himself for not living up to them just as harshly. It doesn't take five minutes to realise what a skilled doctor he is, and Jill from Theatre told me he's a first-rate surgeon.'

Meg clicked her needles and started another row. 'Well, I'll give you that. . .' She gave Anna a wicked grin. 'I do believe you like the man!'

Anna's reply was a shade too prompt. 'I do not! But I do think there's some underlying reason for his abrasiveness,' she said. 'I don't think he's really like that. He's so gentle with the patients, and it's not an act.'

'You mean he just hates nurses!' exclaimed Meg. 'Why?' She nodded knowingly. 'Love-affair gone wrong? Hey, that could be it, Anna. You might have hit on something. Maybe a nurse let him down and now he's taking it out on the rest of us. Trust you to see that—you really ought to have been a psychiatrist!' She added seriously, 'Have you thought any more about going back to medicine?'

Anna swept her hair up and idly knotted it, then pulled the knot undone and let the brown tresses fall to her shoulders again. She shrugged. 'Yes, I've been thinking about it quite a lot, but it's really too late, Meg. I took up nursing instead meaning to stick with it.'

'But really in your heart of hearts you always wanted to study medicine,' insisted Meg. 'You know you still hanker for it. Well, now your mother. . .now you haven't any ties or responsibilities, you could start again and qualify. Why not?'

Anna stared at the fire and pulled her cardigan closer around her. It was growing colder in the room. 'I'm just not sure, Meg, that's why. To start all over again. . . I'm not sure I've got what it takes.'

'Rubbish! Of course you have.'

Anna said, 'I feel so. . .so detached at the moment, Meg.' She laughed ruefully. 'I'm just not used to freedom, I suppose.'

Meg muttered and consulted her knitting pattern. 'Damn, I've done three rows too many without decreasing!'

'Shall I make you a hot drink?' offered Anna, eager to change the subject.

'If you're going to have one. While we drink it, you can tell me everything that happened today. I'm dying to know. Half an hour, that's all. I'm whacked myself.'

'Well, I did doze for an hour earlier,' confessed Anna. 'I was exhausted when I got home, and I was late too.'

While Meg unpicked the surplus rows, Anna made the cocoa and carried the mugs back to the living-room. She told Meg most of what had happened that morning and caused her to laugh a great deal, especially over poor young Liz's predicament.

It was well after midnight when Anna finally slid into bed, but her brain was still active despite the hot drink and the long arduous day. Instead of wakefully brooding over Dr Carroll's brusqueness, however, she found herself worrying about him. Which was ridiculous. He was a grown man, at least thirty, and if something in his personal life was making him difficult to get on with it wasn't her business, and probably he would get over it in due course anyway. She'd better just remember that she wasn't a psychiatrist. Or maybe he *was* a boor, and she was off her head looking for chinks in his armour.

Anna drifted off eventually, and to her dismay overslept. She had forgotten to set her alarm and it was only subconscious programming that woke her. With only five minutes before Dr Carroll would be calling for her, she didn't have a hope of being ready in time. Even as she was belting her dressing-gown around her slim figure, she heard the car horn, and groaned. There was nothing for it but to go out and tell him to go without her. She would call a taxi.

Feeling as small as a cent piece, hair flying, Anna ran down the path to the gate. Dr Carroll, seeing her coming and noticing how she was dressed—or not dressed—got out of the car. He looked her over with more surprise than disapproval.

'What's this? Not ready?'

'I—I overslept,' she said breathlessly. 'I'm sorry. I'll ring and let them know and call a taxi. I'll only be half an hour late. You go.' She wanted to meet those scathing grey eyes bravely, but her courage deserted her and she stared at the mountains beyond his shoulder.

'Can you shower and dress in fifteen minutes?' he asked curtly.

'I—I suppose so.'

'Then I'll wait. Go on! You'll catch your death standing around in the cold. Go and get ready, and be quick about it. No, don't argue. Just get a move on.'

'W-would you like to come in and wait?' she felt obliged to say.

'No, I'll wait in the car,' he decided.

Anna flew back up the path. She had the quickest

shower of her life, and didn't bother with any make-up. Not that she usually used much anyway, as her smooth English skin, which still retained its rosy glow, needed no enhancement, and her eyebrows and eye-lashes were lush enough not to need mascara. Usually she used only a pale lipstick and a touch of eyeshadow in the evenings. She flung her hair into a swirl at the back of her head and hastily filled it with pins to keep it in place, then raced back to the car.

Dr Carroll had evidently gone for a stroll and was striding back to the car as she reached it. She saw binoculars hanging around his neck.

'Some interesting birdlife on the dam back there,' he said, pointing over his shoulder towards the adjacent farmland.

'You enjoy birdwatching?' Anna queried as she got into the passenger seat. She wished it were a topic she knew something about.

'When I get the chance.' He was staring at her again. 'You looked quite different with your hair down.'

She was startled. But of course, the first time she had run down to the car in her dressing-gown her hair had been untidily flying about her shoulders. Neverthe-less, for him to have remarked on it was unexpected, puzzling.

'I assure you I'm still Anna Mackay,' she said, with a smile. 'I didn't ring in my identical twin.'

A sound almost like a chuckle escaped his lips, and Anna felt a strange warmth run through her. 'I'm sorry,' she said again. 'I forgot to set my alarm, and I was rather tired—Meg and I sat up late talking—she doesn't get home until nearly midnight. . .' She broke off. He wasn't interested in her small talk.

'You should have taken a few days off after that

spill,' he said. 'Are you sure you're all right? No nasty headaches or spots before the eyes?'

'Nothing at all. I'm fine. It was probably just that the first day back at work after a holiday is always a bit tiring. One has to get back into gear.'

'You'll find yourself with a new patient this morning,' he told her. 'We had an emergency appendicectomy last night.'

'Oh, so you were called out. Was it the middle of the night?'

'I didn't get to bed until four a.m.' He glanced across at her. 'But I still remembered to set my alarm.'

Anna bit her lip. 'Then you haven't had much sleep. I suppose you could have come in later today if it hadn't been for picking me up.'

'I suppose I could,' he agreed, then added, 'But I probably wouldn't have.'

Their conversation had brought them almost into town. At least the journey was short enough for them not to have to strain to make conversation, Anna thought, but with a feeling almost like regret. A little longer and she might be able to draw him out more. It was a challenge she wouldn't have minded meeting. She might not like the man, but she was none the less intrigued by him.

'I've urged them to hurry up with your new bicycle,' Dr Carroll said as he swung the car through the gates into the staff parking area.

'Thanks.' Anna knew that was for his own sake as much as hers. The sooner she was mobile again, the better, so far as he was concerned.

Once she had left him, she did not see Dr Carroll again that morning, for which she was glad. She had enough problems to cope with without his barging in and picking holes in everything! He was operating all morning, she realised, consulting the lists, and that meant she would have three new patients to accommodate by lunchtime. Thankfully, she noted that they were all routine minor gynaecological cases—two curettages and a tubal ligation. She marvelled at his ability to bounce back after only a couple of hours' sleep.

Last night's appendicectomy, a young woman in her early twenties, was looking cheerful and relieved, but Mrs Gardiner, who had been admitted a few days previously with inflammation of the gall bladder, and who had had a drainage tube inserted, was giving Anna some concern. Her temperature was still high and she was showing signs of toxicity.

Anna called Tom Rolfe, one of the interns, to look at the patient. She would rather have called Dr Carroll, but she could not interrupt his operating schedule.

Tom was reassuring. 'I don't think there's too much to worry about at this stage, but Dr Carroll might want to increase the antibiotic dose.' He smiled at Anna a little flirtatiously. 'I'll tell him if you like.'

'Thanks.' Anna wasn't entirely satisfied, but she couldn't do anything else but keep the patient as comfortable as possible and wait until Dr Carroll could see her.

When he had not put in an appearance by mid-afternoon, she decided she ought to remind him. To her relief he came at once, and as soon as he saw Mrs Gardiner, he drew Anna out into the corridor and rounded on her furiously.

'Why wasn't I called earlier? What sort of a hospital is this? Why do you think we have patients in here? So we can keep an eye on them and treat them promptly——'

Incensed, Anna broke in, 'You were in Theatre this morning——'

'I was through by midday.' Grey eyes blazed at her, but she was not to be annihilated.

'I asked Dr Rolfe to look at her, and he promised to let you know——'

Again he cut her off. 'Well, he didn't. And you should know better than to send verbal messages via other people.' He glared, and Anna glared back. 'It's now half past three.' He tapped his watch for emphasis. 'Surely you must have realised before this that I hadn't got your wretched message?'

'I didn't realise how late it was,' Anna was forced to confess. She added defensively, 'We've been rushed off our feet this afternoon with three new patients, and—and other problems. . .' This time she trailed away, wilting a little under his scorn. She ought to have known better than to make excuses.

'Most of your own making, I don't doubt,' he surmised scathingly.

Hot words rose to her lips, but she swallowed them. There was no point in aggravating him even more.

He stared at her wrathfully for half a minute, then said, 'Well, we'd better see about trying to get her temperature down, hadn't we?'

Anna imagined she heard his teeth grit. 'Yes, Doctor,' she said.

'*I* still think he's probably quite nice underneath,' said Simone later that week, as she and Anna were having lunch together in the staff dining-room. She grinned. 'And I don't mean just what's under that immaculate white coat, suit and underwear!'

For some reason Anna's cheeks flushed a little. It

had never occurred to her to think of Dr Carroll like *that*.

'Not that I don't think he's sexy,' went on Simone dreamily. 'It's funny, but even someone whose guts you hate can stir up the old hormones in spite of it.'

'Well, I haven't noticed any stirring of my hormones,' said Anna emphatically. 'They're quite static where he's concerned.'

Simone sighed. 'What's the use anyway? He doesn't even see us as sex objects like some of the other medicos we have around. Interns—ugh! Who do they think they are, God's gift to nurses?' She groaned over her salad, and, munching a lettuce leaf, said thoughtfully, 'You know, I reckon, away from the hospital, Doc Carroll might be quite a different person. . .but how does one infiltrate his personal life?'

Anna grinned. 'Ask him to go to the cinema with you!'

Simone hooted. 'Can you imagine?' She put on a sultry voice. 'Oh, Doctor, I'm sure you're not sexist, so I was wondering if you'd mind if *I* asked *you* to go and see *Jaws* with me on Saturday night. Of course I'll pay, and buy you a box of chocolates. I'll even drive you home afterwards and give you a goodnight kiss, or maybe——'

'Simone!' hissed Anna, convulsed. 'People can hear you!'

Simone clapped her hand over her mouth. 'Sorry, I forgot I wasn't playing for real.' She gave Anna an inspired look. 'Hey, that would make a good sketch for the hospital revue at Christmas, wouldn't it?'

'You wouldn't dare. He'd recognise himself,' Anna objected.

'Of course he would. That's the whole idea. We take

off the medical staff. They're supposed to be good sports about seeing their foibles lampooned. It's all in good fun.'

Anna had a feeling that Dr Carroll might not see it that way. But she could see that Simone would not be dissuaded. She was a clever actress, especially in comedy sketches, and usually brought the house down. Anna could only hope for a change in Dr Carroll by Christmas that would make taking the mickey out of his crustiness out of date. What *was* he like away from the hospital? she pondered, as she went back to the ward. Like Simone, she was curious, but like Simone she had no chance of ever finding out. If Dr Carroll had a down on nurses for some reason, he was going to steer well clear of them in his personal life.

When, only a couple of days later, Anna received a call from the local bicycle shop, she was surprised and delighted. She had not expected the claim to go through so quickly. Dr Carroll clearly had strings he could pull, which no doubt he was very glad of, she thought, since it meant she was off his conscience all the sooner.

She rang and told him she would not need a lift that evening or the next morning as she would be picking up the new machine after she came off duty, and riding it home.

'Thank you for arranging it,' she said, and could not resist adding, 'You must have quite a bit of clout with your insurance company to have fixed it all up so fast.'

He didn't comment on that, but said admonishingly, 'I hope you'll take more care at the crossroads in future.'

'I'll keep a good look out for *you*, don't worry,'

Anna retorted, then wished she hadn't been so flippant. Speaking to him on the telephone somehow made him seem less intimidating. She'd never have dared to say that to his face. She added hastily, 'I think the cold snap is over. We probably won't get any more black ice on the roads.'

'I hope not.'

'Well, thank you again. . .' Anna felt awkward now.

'You're welcome, Sister.'

How do you end a conversation like this? she thought, feeling jittery all at once. She muttered another few words of appreciation, then said she'd better go, and hung up. She felt it was very abrupt, but what else could she say?

She felt a twinge of conscience when she entered the bicycle shop in the main street of Mount William. The accident had been partly her fault. . .But evidently Dr Carroll's insurance company had been happy to pay up. It was odd that they hadn't required any statement from her about what happened, but since she had never been involved in any such incident before, and she assumed Dr Carroll knew what he was about, she had not thought about it too much.

Bert Turner, the manager of Mount William Cycles, knew Anna slightly since she had been in a few times for items like a new saddle and tyre repair kit and to have her headlamp fixed. He greeted her warmly, and wheeled out the new bicycle.

'How do you like it?' he asked with as much pride as though he'd designed and built it himself.

Anna was rather taken aback. She was no expert, but she could tell it was a more sophisticated model than her old bike, worth more than twice as much. 'It's a beauty,' she said, 'but are you sure? It looks very up-market, and I thought insurance companies only replaced to equal value.'

Bert Turner was quizzical. 'Insurance company?'

'Dr Carroll's insurance company,' Anna explained, surprised at the query. 'They agreed to replace my bike because it was a write-off, but I wasn't expecting such an expensive model.'

Bert shrugged. 'I don't know about that. All I know is that Dr Carroll asked me to get this model. He studied the catalogue and picked it out specially. I had to get it sent up from Melbourne. He said you needed something sturdy and reliable.'

Anna frowned. 'You mean *he* bought it?'

'Right. He was pretty upset about turning your old one into scrap, and insisted you should have the best model available.' He stopped suddenly. 'Hey, maybe I wasn't supposed to tell you that. . .he did say don't make a great fuss about it, just tell her it's OK. Didn't you know he was paying for it himself?'

'No, I didn't, Bert,' said Anna, tight-lipped.

'Well, you should worry,' he said placatingly. 'You've got a smashing new bike, and I dare say he can afford it.'

Anna looked at the bicycle indecisively. I can't take it, she thought. I can't let him do this. . .but Bert was eyeing another potential customer and obviously anxious to leave her. He was waving a piece of paper for her to sign. So she capitulated and signed, and made up her mind to tackle Dr Carroll and insist on paying at least half the cost of the new bicycle.

Outside the store, she climbed on. It took a moment or two to fathom the gears, then she was away. There was no doubt it was a vast improvement on her old model, and she couldn't help being thrilled as she cycled home with extraordinary ease.

The next day she took the bit between her teeth and rang Dr Carroll. She would have gone along to his office personally, but didn't have the courage. As she had previously discovered, talking to him on the phone was marginally easier than face to face.

When she revealed the purpose of her call, he became very curt.

'I don't want to hear another word about it,' he said emphatically. 'You've got your new bike. The matter is closed.'

'But, Dr Carroll, I can't. . .' Anna protested.

'Don't argue, Sister. You've thanked me quite profusely enough already, and quite unnecessarily. I'm sure you have more to do than persisting in trivial discussion about it.'

Anna saw that she was unlikely to win, so she reluctantly acceded and let the matter rest. Meg said, 'So why worry? He's salved his conscience. Don't spoil his warm glow!'

Anna had to accept that. She tried to convince herself that it was all right, really, since he had been in the wrong—well, mostly—and that he had judged the price of the new bike worth it to maintain his no-claims status with his insurance company. If Bert Turner hadn't let the cat out of the bag, she would never have known. But he hadn't had to buy her such an expensive replacement. She wondered why he'd done that.

'So how's it going?' Meg asked Anna one Saturday morning a couple of weeks later, when the two of them happened to have days off coinciding.

Anna poured coffee and pushed a mug across the

kitchen table to Meg. 'How's what going?' she asked innocently.

'You know. Him! Dr Carroll. How are you getting along with him?' Meg asked impatiently, assessing her with a sharp look.

'Oh, him. . .' Anna was gently teasing. 'Fine. . .that is in between times. Do you really want a catalogue of all the things he's found fault with this past fortnight?'

Meg gave a sympathetic groan. 'No, thanks, I can guess. We have to put up with him on Men's Surgical too, you know.' She gave a small sigh. 'I was afraid you might have found a way to tame him, and I was consumed with envy!'

Anna nibbled a digestive biscuit. 'I think he *needs* to find fault. That's the sign of a very insecure person, you know, Meg. Some people can only live with themselves if they can believe that other people have as many or more shortcomings than themselves.'

'You're still into psychoanalysing him?' queried Meg.

'I suppose I am. . .' Anna shrugged. 'But I'm not likely to get to the truth.' She let wondering about the man occupy her thoughts far too much, she knew, but it was hard not to speculate. Something about him still intrigued her.

'Have you thought any more about what you're going to do?' Meg demanded.

'No, I haven't, not really,' Anna confessed. 'It's hard to make decisions, Meg, and so much easier to go on in the same way.'

Meg grew impatient. 'You're not realising your potential, Anna. Nursing is all very well, it's a great career, and you could become a DN or a Matron or whatever, but I don't think that's where your talents lie. Why don't you strike out and do what you really want to do?'

'I don't know. . .' Anna said. 'Maybe I'm scared to rock the boat.'

'Phooey,' said Meg bluntly. 'You just need a shove in the right direction. I wish someone would give it to you. You won't take any notice of me.'

'Give me time. . .'

Meg smiled contritely. 'Yeah, sure. . . I'm sorry, Anna, I shouldn't needle you like that. It's just that I hate to see you. . .' She broke off, biting her lip.

'Wasting my life? Surely I'm not doing that.'

'No. . .oh, forget it, Anna. You'll make your move when the right moment arrives, I'm sure.' Meg changed the subject. 'What's on the agenda this weekend?'

'I'm going bushwalking with the club,' Anna told her. 'You?'

Meg smiled suddenly and radiantly. 'I'm going to a barbecue tomorrow evening with—guess who?'

'Peter Robbins,' said Anna promptly.

'How did you guess?' Meg looked affronted.

Anna laughed. 'You've been dotty about him for months. So he's finally asked you out?' Dr Robbins was a young visiting GP from the town's Banksia Park Medical Centre, very good-looking, rather shy, and a perfect foil for Meg's more outgoing nature. He looked as though he needed mothering, Anna had always thought, and Meg was just the person to oblige. She wished them luck.

Meg was wide-eyed. 'Am I so transparent?'

'Like a window!'

Meg looked dreamily out of the kitchen window towards the mountains. 'He's really awfully nice when you get to know him, Anna.'

'I'm sure.'

Meg breezed on about Peter Robbins and Anna responded as she was expected to, feeling to her surprise a pang of envy. It would be nice to feel the way Meg did about someone, and for that feeling to have some hope of being reciprocated. While she had been responsible for her mother, she had avoided entanglements, knowing that nothing could come of them. But now—now she was free—there wasn't a man in her life she could even fantasise about. Suddenly she felt very lonely.

The feeling was pushed into the background next day, however, when she set off to meet the bushwalking group she had joined when she had first arrived in the Grampians. Always a keen walker, and finding herself drawn to a landscape that in many ways seemed familiar—just the name Grampians had a wonderful liaison with home—Anna had immediately gravitated to the bushwalking club. Nobody else from the hospital, however, was a member, and that was a fact she enjoyed. It was not that she wanted to get away from her colleagues, but it was nice to have an activity she enjoyed that did not involve talking shop.

They always met for the scheduled day's walk at a prearranged spot, where they left cars and bicycles. It had been a five-mile ride for Anna to that day's designated picnic area, but she hadn't minded that. It was the wrong turning she'd taken that had annoyed her, as it cost her all of fifteen minutes to backtrack. As she bowled into the parking area on her new bicycle, she was breathless from pedalling fast, and aware that, judging by the number of cars already parked there, she was indeed late. In her haste, she did not notice a familiar vehicle, and it was only when she hurried up to the group leader with apologies, then looked around at the others, that she saw him.

Her heart sank. Oh, no, she thought, not him! Not Dr Carroll. What's he doing here?

'Anna, you know Scott, I presume,' the leader of the group, Brent Wilson, said casually, waving a hand from one to the other.

Dr Carroll moved to her side. 'Overslept again?' he enquired with a sly glance.

'I miscalculated the time it would take to get here,' Anna said coolly, incensed by his remark. No way was she going to admit to taking a wrong turning.

'Bike behaving OK?' he asked casually.

'Perfectly, thank you.'

There was a glimmer of a smile on his lips. 'If I'd known you were heading this way too, I'd have tooted when you went the wrong way, and saved you being late.'

Anna's face burned. He'd seen her, and she hadn't even realised there was a car behind her. She could have died. If she'd known *he* was going to be here, she'd have turned back for sure! Suddenly the pleasant day out tramping through the sweet-smelling bush had turned into a potential nightmare.

CHAPTER FOUR

SPOILED, Anna thought resentfully as the group set off on the circular walk that would eventually bring them back to the same spot later in the day. A wonderful relaxing Sunday utterly spoiled. How could she relax with Dr Carroll dogging her steps?

It did occur to her that her presence might be as unwelcome to him as his was to her. Maybe he had joined the bushwalking club in order to get away from medical colleagues occasionally. He might have chosen it after he had discovered, as she had, that bushwalking was not a hot favourite recreation among the staff at Mount William Hospital, and, because she had been away on holiday, this was the first time he had encountered her. Yes, she thought, she was probably the last person *he* wanted to see.

There were a dozen people in the group, and realising that she and Dr Carroll knew each other, the rest naturally left them to pair off. Dr Carroll did not know the members of the group very well yet, and that day most of those who had come were people Anna only knew slightly, and most seemed to be in pairs anyway. There was no one she could even pretend to be particularly chummy with, so she found herself walking along side by side with Dr Carroll.

Expecting him to prefer silence to small talk, she forbore to chat, but, trudging along with him only a metre away from her, she felt his proximity intensely, and the antipathy that seemed to flow between them.

She longed for the day to be over. What a pity, she thought, she hadn't lost her way completely and arrived too late to join the walk.

'I suppose you've been walking with the club for quite a while,' Dr Carroll remarked suddenly.

Surprised, Anna answered briefly, 'Oh—yes. I joined soon after I arrived in Mount William. But I don't get to go on their walks all that often.' That ought to reassure him, she thought.

'Does anyone else from the hospital belong?'

'Not that I'm aware of.'

'That was the impression I had,' he answered, sounding to her ears as though he thought he'd been duped.

'You prefer your recreational activities not to include colleagues?' Anna suggested.

He glanced across at her. 'I was wondering the same about you,' he countered smoothly, and she flushed slightly.

With unexpected gallantry, Dr Carroll then remarked, 'I shan't let it spoil *my* enjoyment.'

'Thank you,' murmured Anna, a trifle archly. 'Neither shall I!' She was trying to think of something else to say when she stumbled over an exposed root on the path, but had regained her balance before his outstretched hand reached her. 'You don't *have* to walk with me,' she said. 'If you really want to get completely away from the hospital, I can——'

'We don't have to talk shop, do we?'

She gave him a faint smile. 'We don't have to talk at all.'

He stared at her for a moment, then as they walked on, took what he clearly regarded as a hint and said nothing for the next half-hour. Even then his comment was merely to draw Anna's attention to a bird calling loudly from a clump of acacias. They stopped briefly, and he lent her his binoculars so she could see the white-plumed honeyeater more clearly.

'I ought to get some binoculars,' she said, handing them back. 'I never realised what a difference they make to looking at birds. You can actually see their eyes, and the plumage is quite different.'

Dr Carroll laughed softly, and said, 'Things are not always what they seem.' And his eyes met hers for an instant, searchingly, as though his enigmatic remark was meant to refer to her. It might well refer to him, she thought. It was a disconcerting moment, and she walked quickly on.

A short time later they paused again, this time to admire the vivid gold and black plumage of a male golden whistler. When Dr Carroll slipped the strap of the binoculars over Anna's neck, his fingers brushed her nape and caused a tingling warmth to circulate through her, as though she had touched a live wire. This didn't please her at all.

They dawdled for several minutes, and, realising how far behind they were, she said, 'We'd better catch up. We won't be popular if we get lost.' There was an odd little quaver in her voice which didn't please her either.

Dr Carroll looked startled, as though he'd forgotten all about the others. He took back his binoculars and they marched on, increasing their speed to catch up with the main group. This proved easy enough, since the group had stopped for morning tea. To Anna's embarrassment there was some gentle ribbing when they showed up, a few knowing winks and smiles, as though they had hung back on purpose. Anna felt annoyed, since nothing could have been further from the truth. She moved around the group away from Dr Carroll and chatted to other bushwalkers, determined now to avoid the registrar for the rest of the hike.

But it was not to be so easy. The rest of the group had paired them off, and paired off they were doomed to remain. Anna set off in the midst of the group, but soon found herself bringing up the rear side by side with Dr Carroll again, although she was not too sure how it had happened.

They stopped for lunch at the base of a waterfall. Sunlight slanted through the trees, and out of the wind it was comparatively warm. Anna shed her backpack and unzipped her parka. She sat on a rock and stretched out her legs. It was very peaceful. The noise of the waterfall drowned out conversations and the bush smelt wonderfully fresh and clean, a mingling of eucalyptus, wattle blossom and earth mould.

The leader and a couple of the men, including Dr Carroll, gathered wood and lit a small fire in the stone fireplace against the cliff face. A billy was set to boil and the aroma of woodsmoke for a time overpowered the other perfumes of the bush.

Anna, sitting slightly apart from the main group, found her eyes drawn to Dr Carroll, watching his every movement, and, although she tried not to, she couldn't help wondering about him. Once he glanced across at her and caught her staring. She looked away quickly and took a bite of her sandwich. She pretended to be intent on something in a tree—too intent. A moment later, the doctor joined her.

'Anything interesting?' he queried.

'I don't know. It flew away.' She answered coolly, wishing he would go away and talk to someone else, but he sprawled on the rock near her and began eating his lunch.

'Pleasant spot,' he remarked, as Anna wondered if he had made the rather untidy sandwiches himself. She knew that instead of occupying accommodation in town provided by the hospital he had opted to rent a house which was even more isolated than the one she and Meg shared. So far as anyone knew, he lived alone, so she presumed he must have.

'Lovely. So peaceful. . .'

One corner of his mouth tilted slightly. 'Except for the human chatter?' Laughter came from across the clearing, and momentarily voices were sharply clear on the still air.

Anna nodded mutely, unable to prevent a smile escaping.

'I shan't utter another word,' he whispered, mocking her a little.

Like him, she leaned back and gazed at the sky. His manner was such a far cry from the abrasiveness she always expected from him at the hospital that she felt quite companionable with him.

She was miles away when the call came to set off again. Reluctantly she screwed up her lunch papers, flicked the last drops of tea out of her mug and stowed everything back in her backpack. Out of the corner of her eye she saw Dr Carroll doing likewise. They hoisted their backpacks over their shoulders and were ready to go when the others were.

'We have to cross the creek here,' the leader announced, 'so take care.'

One by one the party forded the fast-flowing creek at the foot of the waterfall by using stepping-stones. Anna found herself again at the rear with Dr Carroll.

She hesitated on the edge of the creek, not sure which foot to put first. Dr Carroll strode easily across and then held out his hand.

Anna, feeling independent, ignored it and stepped tentatively on to the first stepping-stone. Her next step was firm, but the last stone had a patch of moss on it and her foot slipped. Sure she was going to fall, she spread her arms wide, and found herself steadied by a strong grip on one wrist. Dr Carroll jerked her to the bank where he was standing with such force that she came violently up against him, which almost knocked the breath out of her.

His arm slid around her as momentarily they rocked perilously, and then, shockingly, she was held fast and he was looking into her face with an unmistakable intention in his grey eyes. A sudden breeze along the valley drifted a fine spray from the waterfall over them and misted the bush so that they seemed cocooned in a passing cloud. As the other bushwalkers disappeared from view, the only sound was the piping of a spinebill deep in the undergrowth.

Dr Carroll's lips met Anna's before she was aware they were going to. She was conscious of a soft warmth, a slight moistness, and then a hard pressure as he kissed her with a fervour that set her senses reeling, and sent a warm melting sensation through her whole body, evoking an involuntary response. She capitulated only for seconds, then the craziness of what was happening hit her and she jerked herself away from him.

'Dr Carroll!' Her indignation sounded thin and forced.

He was smiling an odd tilted half-smile, and looked mildly surprised himself. Now, even more, he was not the Dr Carroll she recognised, and she didn't know what to do or say. He murmured, 'Off duty, it would sound friendlier if you called me Scott and allowed me to call you Anna.'

Anna swallowed. She still didn't know what to say, how to cope with the situation. And meanwhile, she realised, the rest of the party must be getting further and further ahead. Any minute now they would be missed and someone sent back to find them.

'We'd better hurry,' she said, trying to iron the tremble out of her voice. 'The others will be miles ahead of us.' She began to scramble up the incline in the direction the rest of the party had taken.

He caught her hand and halted her. 'Are you angry?' The anxiety in his grey eyes confused her. She was not accustomed to this new, different Dr Carroll. It was too sudden.

She jerked her hand from his. 'Of course I'm not! What's there to be angry about in a few hormones overworking?' She fled on as fast as she could, and he did not detain her again, but followed her up the steep track to the top of the cliffs. Both were too breathless from climbing to speak.

There were no nods and winks this time from the rest of the bushwalkers when they caught up with them. Anna longed for the walk to be over, and yet, perversely, she felt an odd kind of pleasure trudging along beside Dr Carroll—Scott. . . She'd never be able to bring herself to call him that, she thought, not even off duty. It amused her to think that probably neither of them would go bushwalking again in case the other was there. Perhaps she should graciously offer to be the one to give it up, and if she did, would he show that streak of gallantry again and insist that he took up another activity since she had been in the club longer than he?

Neither happened. That Dr Carroll was definitely unpredictable Anna discovered yet again when they all arrived back at the picnic spot where their cars and bikes were parked. In spite of the tensions, she had enjoyed the walk, and although she felt flushed and slightly breathless after the last kilometre uphill she also felt exhilarated. It was growing late and a bank of dark clouds had come up during the past half-hour. Now it began to rain. Anna pulled up the hood on her parka and was fastening the strings when Dr Carroll came over to her.

'I can sling your bike on the roof-rack and give you a lift, if you like,' he offered.

She shook her head. 'No, really. . .thanks, but I'm all right. It's only a shower.'

He glanced at the purple-black mass of cloud looming over the mountain behind them. 'I don't think so. We're in for a storm, by the look of that sky. You'd better be sensible and come with me.'

'I've ridden in the rain before,' she said stubbornly, as thunder rolled ominously in the distance.

He was not to be put off. 'If you had an accident I'd have you on my conscience again.'

The leader, Brent Wilson, joined them. 'Nice to see you again, Scott—you too, Anna. Great you two know each other.' He pulled his own hood further over his forehead. 'Looks like a storm coming up. You giving Anna a ride, Scott? I can if you can't, but I've already got one bike on the rack.'

'I'll take care of Anna,' Scott Carroll said firmly, and Anna knew she would have no further say in the matter. She capitulated graciously.

While Dr Carroll lashed her bicycle to the roof-rack, she made herself comfortable in the passenger seat of his car. There were occasional flashes of lightning and the thunder was louder. The other cars were all leaving the parking area, and, being at the end furthest from the exit, they were once again bringing up the rear.

As they drove back towards the main road, it began to rain heavily, almost too heavily for the windscreen-wipers to cope. Watching the water sloshing off the bonnet and splashing up in muddy waves from the car's front bumper and wheels, Anna was thankful she had accepted the lift.

'I'm glad I'm not out in this,' she said at last, shivering. 'Thank you very much for the lift, Dr Carroll.'

'Scott,' he reminded her, glancing at her in quite a friendly way. 'It isn't difficult to pronounce.'

'Sorry—I'm just not used to it. . .'

'Are you warm enough? Would you like the heating up a bit?'

'No, thanks, I'm fine.'

Anna subsided into an uneasy silence again. She could not deny she was enjoying his solicitude, and at the moment his abrasive manner seemed almost unbelievable. But, she warned herself, she must not enjoy his company too much. Tomorrow he would doubtless revert to being his normal self. Or was this gentler mood the normal one? She stole a quick glance at his profile as he concentrated on avoiding the worst pot-holes. It was a strong face, with slightly jutting chin and firm jawline, a straight nose and deep-set eyes. His dark hair was tousled from having been under the hood, and was plastered against his forehead. His lips were firmly together, suggesting gritted teeth, as he battled to keep control of the car on the muddy track, made worse by the recent passage of all the other vehicles.

At the T-junction where the bush road joined the macadam, Scott Carroll let out a grunt of relief as he swung the car to the right. Anna hated to do it, but she had to speak.

'Dr Carr. . .Scott, I think we should have turned left,' she said. 'Mount William is that way.' She smiled a little, as she jerked her thumb in the opposite direction, wondering how he would take it. As for herself, she felt much better about having taken a wrong turning that morning. It was reassuring to find that Scott Carroll wasn't infallible.

He did not slow down. 'I know.'

Anna was now nonplussed. 'But I don't understand. Why aren't we going back to Mount William?' She glanced at him in some alarm.

'Don't worry, I'm not kidnapping you. But as it's so late, I thought we might get tea in Winston. There's a charming little pub there that serves the kind of meals bushwalkers need after a long hike. Hungry?'

Was he never going to stop surprising her? Anna swallowed hard and said, 'Well, yes, but. . .'

He negotiated a sharp bend. 'Your reluctance isn't very flattering to my ego!'

A flush warmed her skin. 'I'm sorry. But I wasn't expecting. . .' As she spoke she reminded herself that she hadn't been expecting that kiss by the waterfall either. Was this a preliminary to testing her responses again? A ghastly thought occurred to her. Was Scott Carroll a frustrated male who was hoping——?

Her thought was cut off as she slammed forward

against her seat-belt as the car braked suddenly. She glimpsed a large kangaroo bounding off into the bush.

Scott seemed a little shaken too. 'Near miss,' he said, and Anna noticed that his knuckles were white. He looked at her anxiously. 'Sorry about that. Are you all right?'

'Yes, of course.'

'I hope you won't have belt bruises tomorrow. That was a hard jolt I gave you.'

'It wasn't your fault, and I'm glad you missed the 'roo.'

The low cloud had brought an early dusk and before they reached the small town of Winston headlights were needed. There was no further incident, and by the time they turned into the hotel car park the rain had eased off.

'I must ring Meg,' said Anna, as they entered the long low bluestone building. 'She'll worry if I'm not home when she expects me, especially in this weather.' While Dr Carroll strolled into the bar, she found a phone and made her call. Meg had already gone out, so she left a message on the answering machine, hoping Meg would check the tape when she got home if it was before she arrived herself. Otherwise there could be a search party out for her!

While she had the opportunity, she headed for the ladies and combed her hair, which had become rather tangled. She pinned it back into a tidy knot and wished she could powder her nose, but she never took make-up when she went bushwalking. Her skin glowed from the day's exertion and there was a sparkle in her eyes that even she could see. But it would have been nice to tone down that faint shine on her nose! Not that it mattered, of course. She wasn't trying to impress Scott Carroll. Heaven forbid!

When she joined him in the bar, Dr Carroll had a tankard of beer before him. He had removed his parka and looked even more handsome than usual in a polo-neck tan sweater and brown corduroys. The sweater accentuated his arm and chest muscles, and as he stood up she noticed how slim his waist and hips were. Lean and strong, she thought, then warned herself not to admire his physique too much.

'The walk seems to have done you good,' he remarked softly. 'You look a picture of glowing health.'

As his gaze drifted down over her close-fitting green skivvy, Anna's colour deepened. She clasped her hands to her burning face. 'Coming into the warmth out of the cold air always makes my face tingle.'

Scott Carroll chuckled and caught hold of her arm. 'A drink? And then we'll eat. I don't know about you, but I'm ravenous!' He ordered a glass of red wine for her and they found a table, then went across to the smorgasbord which offered both hot dishes and salads.

There were a few people in the bar, but no one Anna recognised, although people in this area used the Mount William Hospital. She guessed that the registrar patronised the place because he was not so likely to be recognised here. He would hardly want to be seen eating out with her in Mount William. That would cause gossiping tongues to wag. It was even a risk here that someone they knew would choose tonight to drive to Winston. She had never been to the pub before and was surprised it was not better known among her colleagues.

'This place must be one of the year's best kept secrets,' she remarked as they carried their food to their table, which was not too close to the crackling wood fire in an enormous grate. 'How did you find out about it?'

'Just nosing around. I get the impression that most of the staff at the MWH stick in and around the town even though it's a bit short on good restaurants. The pubs are quite good, though.'

'There's a really nice restaurant a few miles out of town,' Anna told him. 'A converted farmhouse. It's very popular with the MWH crowd, but if you prefer to go where you're not likely to meet any of them this is a better bet, I'd say.'

One dark eyebrow quirked. 'I suppose you think I'm very unsociable.'

She kept her expression non-committal. 'There's no obligation to mix business with pleasure.'

'The food is good here,' Scott Carroll said, as though that was sufficient defence.

'I won't spread the good news back at the MWH,' she promised, and earned a slightly wry grin from him but no further comment.

Tucking into her enormous vegetable-filled filo pastry over which she had poured lashings of home-made tomato sauce, Anna agreed with his opinion of the food. While they ate, there was a long silence, during which she wondered several times whether there was going to be any conversation at all, and if so what about. She was sure he wouldn't welcome shop talk and even surer he would not want to answer personal questions. She was loath to start chattering herself, so she waited for Scott to speak.

But when the silence seemed to be extending interminably, and she could stand it no longer, she ventured, 'Back there in the bush, you sounded like an expert on birds. Have you been birdwatching long?'

Scott's eyes rose to her face as though he'd forgotten she was sitting opposite him. He had been miles away, she realised, in some private world of his own. She longed to ask him why he had come to Mount William, whether he was married, all kinds of personal things, but she didn't dare. Those might be the normal questions you would ask someone you worked with, but not Dr Carroll. Anna felt she had established a tenuous rapport with him today, and she was not going to risk ruining it by being nosy.

'Since I was about ten years old,' he answered. 'It's a fascinating hobby. I go out most weekends, or any other spare time I have—mostly to the Dandenongs when I'm in Melbourne. Up here, there's a wealth of birdlife in the Grampians, and I find it very relaxing watching bird behaviour.'

Anna suppressed her desire to know more about him personally, and asked what she hoped were intelligent questions about birds. It must have been obvious that her knowledge was very scanty, but Scott seemed delighted to inform her, and she had to admit he made the subject very interesting and entertaining, and to her delight the humorous side of him surfaced once or twice.

They finished the meal with coffee and a liqueur, and after the second cup of coffee, Scott said, 'If you've finished, shall we go?' All at once he seemed to be in a hurry. He rose and shrugged into his parka, then deftly helped Anna on with hers.

The rain had gone and the sky was clear and starry. There was a sharp bite in the night air, but it was warm in the car. They did not talk much, and what conversation they did have was mainly still about birds or bushwalking.

Anna was still bewildered by the whole thing. She was well aware already that Dr Scott Carroll was an impetuous man, but his behaviour this evening puzzled her. Why had he taken her to the pub for a meal? Had that been his intention when they left the picnic area, or had he thought of it on the spur of the moment to cover his taking a wrong turning? Thinking it over, she felt more and more that covering up had been his only reason. He had lumbered himself with her because he didn't want to admit to an error.

When he drew up outside the house she shared with Meg, Anna said, 'That was very pleasant, Scott. Thank you very much for the meal.' His name slipped off her tongue more easily now.

'My pleasure,' he said, then took her completely by surprise by asking, 'How do you like living in Australia?'

Since he had not asked her any personal questions before, Anna was taken aback. 'Very much.'

He leaned back comfortably, half facing her, as though settling down for a conversation. 'Do you think you'll stay here permanently?' The car light cast shadows on his face, emphasising his strong jawline and broad forehead, but hiding any expression in his eyes.

'I don't know. . .' The unexpectedness of his interest caught her off guard and made her feel confused. It was a funny time to start such a conversation. It occurred to her that maybe he felt remiss for talking too much about his interest in birdwatching and not enough about her. Anna did not want to go into too many details, so she said briefly, 'My mother died a couple of months ago, and I'm—well, at a sort of crossroads, I suppose. I'm not sure what I want to do next.'

He murmured a brief condolence, all the time looking at her steadily, then asked, 'Why did you come out in the first place?'

Anna shrugged, still reluctant to go into details. He couldn't really be interested. But she had to say something. 'My mother was a widow and after she had a stroke back in England she wanted to come out here to be near my brother, so we emigrated. But eighteen months ago he and his family went off to Canada. Mum didn't want to move again, so we stayed here, and then she had another stroke—a fatal one.' Anna's eyes filled with tears, which appalled her. She didn't want Dr Carroll to see her cry.

He said gently, 'I'm sorry. You've obviously had a hard time recently.' He paused, still looking intently at her. 'I can understand your indecision. Now you're free and can do whatever you want, you're not sure what that is. Am I right?'

Suddenly it felt claustrophobic in the car, but Anna could not find the will or the excuse to escape quickly. Talking was the best way to keep control of her feelings, so she rushed into telling him how she had started her medical course in England, but had switched to nursing after her mother's stroke.

He looked astonished. 'You wanted to be a doctor?' His surprise was tinged with admiration. 'And you gave it up and became a nurse because of your mother?'

Anna felt uncomfortable. 'It wasn't possible to train as a doctor where we lived in England, but I was able to do nursing. It seemed like the ideal alternative at the time.'

'That was very noble of you,' he said, without sounding patronising.

She shrugged. 'Not really. I like nursing. And I didn't have any choice, anyway.'

He regarded her thoughtfully for a moment or two. 'Why not take up where you left off now?'

Anna lifted her shoulders indecisively. 'That's what Meg keeps urging me to do, but I'm too old—and medical courses are long. . .'

He scoffed, 'You've got a lifetime ahead of you. Plenty of time to qualify.'

She smiled, but did not comment. 'Well, now you know all about me,' she said lightly. 'I don't know much about you, though.'

Abruptly, she felt his withdrawal, so she was hardly surprised when instead of the reciprocal enlightenment she had foolishly hoped for, he said, 'Yes, it was a pleasant day, and an even pleasanter evening. Thank you for your company, Anna.' She was no nearer finding out anything about him than she had been before.

'Yes. . .thank you again,' she muttered, and opened the car door.

'I'll see you safely to your door,' he offered.

She protested, 'No, really, it's all right. The porch light is on. Meg's home. . .'

'Sure?'

'Yes—don't get out. Please. . .' Suddenly she felt embarrassed.

'Goodnight, then, Anna.'

'Goodnight.' She slammed the passenger door shut and ran up the path to the porch, aware that he lingered to make sure she reached it safely. She turned and lifted her hand in a wave of acknowledgement, knowing he would see her in the light from the porch lamp, and then as the car sped away she clapped a hand over her mouth.

'Oh, no! My bike!'

Dr Scott Carroll had just driven off with her bicycle still firmly lashed to the roof-rack of his car. What an idiot he'd think her to have forgotten it. But he'd forgotten it too, she reminded herself defensively as she let herself into the house. It wasn't just her fault.

CHAPTER FIVE

IT WASN'T all that late, but Anna tiptoed into the house in case Meg had gone to bed. Her friend, however, was ironing in the kitchen. She looked relieved to see Anna.

'Oh, there you are!'

'Did you get my message?' asked Anna. 'I rang about six.'

Meg nodded. 'As you weren't home, I had a feeling you might have rung, so I checked the tape.' She paused, iron in hand. 'Where were you? There was a lot of background noise.'

Anna's message had been cryptic: not to worry, she was having a meal out and would be home later. Meg's face said more than her query. What she really wanted to know was, who with? Anna hesitated, reluctant all at once to tell her the truth. Meg wouldn't gossip, but she would start speculating, and really there was nothing to speculate about. She had also promised to protect Dr Carroll's favourite eating spot. So, convincing herself it was all in a good cause, she said,

'I went out for a meal after the walk.'

To her surprise and relief, Meg did not enquire precisely with whom or where, assuming no doubt that it must have been with the bushwalking group. But Anna realised immediately that she might have put her foot in it. What if Scott came back with her bike tonight, or Meg saw him when he returned it tomorrow morning? How was she going to explain that away?

She crossed her fingers, hoping he'd choose to return it in the morning when, with any luck, Meg would be still in bed and need never know.

'How was the barbecue?' she asked, hoping Meg's outing had been eventful enough to eclipse her own. 'Was Peter up to expectations?'

Meg gave a dreamy sigh. 'Fabulous! It was a great party, and we got on really well. It's the first time we've ever talked really deeply about anything. I never imagined we'd have so much in common!'

Anna laughed. 'Deep talk at a party? That sounds serious!' She added, 'Did you get that storm we had this afternoon?'

'No, luckily we didn't. We could see the sky darkening over the mountains, but it was fine where we were most of the time. A couple of light showers, that's all. Not that it mattered—we were only outside for a little while cooking our food. We were indoors most of the time.'

'Did Peter ask you out again?'

Meg beamed. 'Yes, he did.' She slammed the iron on the stand. 'Anna, I'm just scared to even think about him—I've never felt this way before. . .'

'Sounds like love.'

'If it isn't—I'll *die*!' Meg whispered.

Anna smiled indulgently. 'I doubt it! You'll survive and so will he, and in the fullness of time wedding bells will ring throughout the land!'

Meg said soberly, 'I didn't imagine I'd ever feel like this, Anna. I've never felt this way about anyone else.' She grinned apologetically. 'Sorry, you're tired and wanting to go to bed. You don't want to listen to all this crazy rambling. I'm off to bed myself anyway.'

'Sweet dreams,' Anna wished for her.

Involuntarily, she yawned. She was tired, but she was afraid to go to bed before Meg just in case Scott did take it into his head to come back that night. As Meg was about to fold the ironing-board up, Anna said, 'Leave it, Meg. I've got a couple of things I want to press.'

Meg's head was too much in the clouds for her to be surprised. She said goodnight and went off with her pile of ironing, and presumably she would enoy sweet dreams, Anna thought with a pang of envy.

Anna did her own unnecessary ironing, and hung about until she was sure Meg was in bed, and she felt it was unlikely that Scott would return that night, before she went to bed herself. She was dead tired after the long walk and the emotional tension of the evening, and she slept soundly.

One thing she did not forget to do, and that was to set her alarm. In the morning, she hurried her shower, dressed quickly and rushed breakfast, wanting to be sure to be quite ready by the time Scott arrived as she expected he would. Thank goodness Meg, as usual, was dead to the world still and not likely to catch her out.

Anna made sure she was hovering on the veranda well before she expected Scott to arrive so that he would see her and not blast his horn, which might just penetrate Meg's consciousness and make her curious later. Deception, Anna thought, was really not for her. She was the kind to make a fatal slip-up, forget her story, or feel perpetually guilty.

She had a glimpse of the road from the veranda, so spotted Scott Carroll's car before it reached the house and she was at the front gate as he pulled up. Her bicycle was still on the roof-rack.

He got out and said very drily, 'You forgot your bike.'

As though it had been entirely her fault! Anna said, 'Sorry. It wasn't until you'd driven off that I realised. . .'

'I didn't think there was much point in coming back last night.'

'No—I'm glad you didn't. . .' Anna felt more and more foolish with every minute. 'I'm sorry you had to make a detour this morning. I feel so stupid walking off like that, forgetting it.'

He made no polite disclaimer as most people would have done, but heaved her bicycle on to the verge and propped it against the fence.

Anna said, 'Thank you.' She couldn't use his first name. He seemed so different again this morning, more his old distant self. Scott, the man who had thawed a little yesterday, had gone again and Dr Carroll was back. He was naturally annoyed with her for forgetting the bicycle. After all, it was hers, and her place to remember it, not his. She said, 'I feel such a fool forgetting it.'

He gave her a long appraisal from steely grey eyes. 'Well, so long as you're not as absent-minded on the job.'

That was enough to goad her, but she resisted the urge to retort in kind, and repeated her thanks.

He looked her over with clinical impartiality. 'Well, I suppose you want to get started. I won't hold you up.' And, with a muttered goodbye, he departed.

Anna watched the car out of sight, then mounted her bicycle and set off. She felt terribly deflated.

* * *

'It's going to be one of those weeks,' predicted Simone, a little later that same morning. 'Mark my words.'

Anna tried to sound more optimistic even if she didn't feel it. 'Come on, it's not that bad. Just because we had three emergencies admitted over the weekend.'

'And Mrs Bryant,' Simone reminded her darkly.

Anna groaned in agreement. 'Yes—well, I suppose we could do without her. But every hospital has them, Simone, the moaners and groaners, the patients you can't do anything right for.'

Mrs Bryant was a regular, an elderly woman who seemed to have everything under the sun wrong with her. She had been in for at least half a dozen different operations, and occasionally had been admitted to the medical ward too. It was hardly her fault, and she wasn't a hypochondriac, but she was a complainer, which could get the nursing staff down at times, especially busy times when every second bell seemed to be Mrs Bryant requiring attention.

'And young Liz who can't do anything right, stop!' laughed Simone, who was much less gloomy in temperament than she sometimes seemed.

'She'll straighten out all of a sudden,' said Anna, but without total conviction. 'She's still nervous, that's the trouble.'

'Which is why she is at this moment changing flowers and tidying bedclothes,' said Simone. 'I know she ought to be doing something more—well, medical, but I felt more secure with her doing harmless duties.'

'She has to get experience,' Anna reproved. 'That's the only way to learn.'

'But she needs constant supervision, and I haven't had time this morning,' said Simone. 'Even our fool-proof new autoclave packed up when she was using it.'

As she spoke, there was a rattle at the door, which burst open to admit an anxious Liz.

'What's the matter, Liz?' Anna asked kindly, not too alarmed by her stricken expression, since it was almost permanently on the girl's face.

Liz gasped, 'It's Mrs Henderson! She's making a dreadful noise. I don't think she can breathe properly. She looks very cy-cyanosed. . .' She looked at the two seniors as though expecting a reprimand.

Anna and Simone did not hesitate. They both rushed to the ward to check on the patient.

'She was all right half an hour ago,' Simone said.

Anna took one look at Mrs Henderson and rapped out, 'Get the oxygen, Simone, and ask someone to call Dr Carroll. Emergency!'

The patient, who had been admitted with severely fractured ribs after a car accident at the weekend, was in dire distress. The blue tinge in her skin indicated a serious depletion of oxygen to the blood. She had slipped down the bed a little, and at first glance she appeared to be unconscious, but her eyelids flickered when she realised someone was bending over her, and she tried to speak.

'Don't try to talk,' said Anna, 'it's all right—you'll be fine shortly, just as soon as we get some oxygen for you.'

'I'm—dying. . .' rasped the woman frantically.

'No, you're not,' soothed Anna. 'I know it feels terrible at the moment, but in a few seconds. . .' She slid her arms under the patient's shoulders. 'It'll be better when you're sitting up. As you were before.'

Mrs Henderson coughed and retched, and flecks of sputum stained the sheet. Anna was perturbed to see blood in it. What was keeping Simone, for heaven's sake? And then Simone was there with a mask and cylinder. Anna quickly fitted the mask to the patient's mouth and nose, and watched the oxygen inflate the cuff. There was an almost immediate alleviation of Mrs Henderson's distress, which Anna noted with relief, although she knew the underlying condition was probably serious.

A voice at her elbow said, 'This is your emergency?'

She turned, with a new kind of relief, to see Scott Carroll. Somewhere in the recesses of her brain something else more personal registered too, but now was not the moment to identify it.

'Yes. She collapsed a few minutes ago.'

'She's not one of my patients,' said Scott. 'One of the weekend casualties?'

Anna nodded. 'Car accident on Saturday night—crushed ribs and multiple bruises. I suspect there's air or maybe blood in the pleural cavity. . .' She broke off. It wasn't her role to diagnose. She stood aside while the registrar examined the patient, gently reassuring her, and saying nothing to Anna.

He eventually acknowledged that Anna was still there, by frowning at her. He drew back a little and said in a low voice, 'I think a tracheostomy is called for, don't you? It should have been done yesterday.' Judging by his grim expression, someone was going to get a rocket over that, Anna thought.

She was astonished by the 'don't you?' Why was he asking her? True, she had told him she had commenced medical studies and given them up, but she wasn't sure how to take his remark. It was an odd moment to mock.

'Yes, I imagine so,' she muttered.

He glowered at her. 'You *imagine*? In medicine, Sister, you do not imagine. You make decisions.'

Anna lifted her eyes to his. 'Yes, I do think a tracheostomy is the correct procedure to follow,' she stated firmly, and caught a startled look from Simone, who was diligently monitoring the oxygen.

'Then you'd better alert the operating-room immediately, and prepare Mrs Henderson for emergency surgery.' Scott glanced quickly from Anna to Simone and back to Anna. 'You are familiar with nursing patients after tracheostomies?'

'Yes, of course,' said Anna, and Simone nodded.

He gave a grim little smile. 'Then there shouldn't be any problems, should there?' His eyes rested on Anna's face for a moment, then he left them.

Simone sighed. 'What have we done to deserve him?'

Anna shrugged. She didn't want to discuss Dr Carroll, and, besides, there was too much to do. She vowed to do her utmost to make sure that Scott would not be able to find fault with the post-operative nursing of Mrs Henderson.

After Mrs Henderson had been taken to the operating-room, Anna set Fran and Liz to prepare the small side-ward which they used for cases needing to be specialled. Dr Carroll was going to ask for twenty-four-hour nursing care, she felt certain, to ensure that no further problems arose, or that if they did there was someone competent on hand. Anticipating the patient's needs, she supervised the setting up of an apparatus trolley which would remain in the room in case of urgent need at any time, and the installation of a respirator, and checked the availability of oxygen.

In between times she answered calls and assisted

other nurses with minor problems in the wards, of
which there seemed to be more than usual that day.

'Oh, no, not Mrs Bryant *again*!' she exploded, when
Fran came to fetch her because Mrs Bryant insisted on
seeing the sister in charge.

Not wanting to be away from the ward when Mrs
Henderson returned from Theatre, Anna skipped
lunch. She was persuaded to pause briefly to snatch a
cup of coffee and a large slice of her favourite fruit
cake by Liz who, showing unexpected perception, had
insisted on getting the snack for her from the canteen,
when Dr Carroll burst into her office. His eyes swept
across her and her snack with undisguised disapproval.

'I expected someone to be on hand to receive Mrs
Henderson back,' he said icily. 'Isn't that usual for
cases coming to you from Theatre?'

Caught with her mouth full of fruit cake, Anna was
unable to reply instantly. She chewed and swallowed
hastily. 'She's back?' It was hard to remain unruffled
under the icy glare of deep-set grey eyes. A morsel of
cake crumb stuck in her throat and she coughed. She
took a swig of coffee to dislodge it, feeling her face
redden as she did so, partly from the effort of not
coughing and partly from annoyance.

'I came up with her myself,' the registrar said.

Anna gained control of herself. 'Nobody notified us.'

His eyes narrowed as though he didn't believe her.
She refused to be quelled, although she felt at a distinct
disadvantage. 'If I'd known you were on your way with
Mrs Henderson, would I be sitting here and. . .?' But
words failed her, as they often did in the face of his
steely stare.

He seemed to consider what she'd said, and when he
spoke again, his tone was a shade less accusatory.

'Maybe one of your nurses took the message and didn't tell you,' he allowed. 'That girl Liz whatever her name is is a bit of a scatterbrain.'

Anna rose. 'I've been in my office for the past ten minutes or so. Maybe they just forgot to ring through from Recovery.'

His eye drifted over her cup and saucer and the half-eaten fruit cake. 'I'm glad some people can find time to stop for a cuppa and a slice of cake,' he said drily.

Anna felt a surge of anger and almost blew up. 'I didn't have time for lunch,' she told him in a clipped tone. 'One of my nurses very kindly fetched me the coffee and cake, and I could hardly offend her by not eating it. She was thinking of my welfare!'

He was unimpressed. 'I missed lunch too,' he said pointedly. And then, 'Well, if you've finished, perhaps we can make Mrs Henderson comfortable.'

Anna hadn't finished, but that was a minor point. She was there to do his bidding, and looking after patients came before one's own welfare, even when one was exhausted. And she was close to exhaustion, she realised. She had been on her feet all day, rushing hither and yon, but it wasn't all physical. Part of it was frayed nerves caused by the doctor now at her side. It wasn't just his abrasive manner either. Scott Carroll was a thorn in her side, to be sure, but he was also a disturbing presence in her subconscious, as well as in her office. Incredibly, as their eyes met, there was a spontaneous spark between them that was anything but antipathy. Anna, shocked to the core, lowered her eyes. Now she really was imagining things. When she glanced up she saw only a familiar withdrawal in his expression.

'We've got Room Five ready for her,' she said, and

led the way with as much self-control as she could
muster.

Dr Carroll looked around the room where Mrs
Henderson would be receiving twenty-four-hour care
for the next couple of days at least, and Anna held her
breath as she waited for him to find something wrong,
some piece of equipment lacking, some detail forgotten. But he said nothing. He and the theatre technician
who had brought the patient in carefully transferred
her into the bed. She was semi-conscious now and
moaning a little.

It took only a short time to connect up the respirator
and adjust the air flow through the tracheostomy tube
in the patient's throat. Anna was pleased to find that
everything worked smoothly and not a single complaint
came from Dr Carroll.

She gave him her full attention when he issued
instructions, and, when he rapped out a few questions
on how she would care for the artificial opening in the
patient's throat and ensure that there were no problems
with the oxygen flow, she answered confidently and
accurately.

To her amazement he said, 'Thank you, Sister. It
sounds as though you know what you're doing.' He
included Simone in his glance, and she looked equally
surprised.

He motioned Anna to accompany him when he left,
and outside in the corridor he said, 'Don't hesitate to
call me if there's any problem. I expect a blockage may
occur later that may need suction to relieve it. Tell
whoever takes over from you that she must call me or
another doctor immediately if there's the slightest sign
that the airway is becoming congested.'

'Yes, I'll do that,' said Anna. He did not leave her,

but stood looking at her, his expression preoccupied, so she asked, 'Is there anything else?'

'No. You can go back and enjoy your tea and cakes now.' He turned on his heel and marched away, leaving her fuming.

The coffee was of course stone cold, but she drank it, and mopped up the remaining cake and crumbs. 'Just because *he's* a martyr,' she muttered.

The rest of the day was no less hectic for Anna. With regular checks on Mrs Henderson, supervising other patient treatments, and dealing with the usual pile of paperwork, she scarcely paused for a minute, and was in fact late going off duty after taking extra time to brief the sister taking over from her on Mrs Henderson's condition.

She arrived home completely wrung out, made herself a couple of sandwiches and a pot of tea, then went straight to bed. She was asleep almost as soon as her head touched the pillow and she did not wake until her alarm went off next morning.

It was an effort to pedal to work and, despite having slept well, she felt as though she had not really rested. She felt thoroughly frayed at the edges, and also depressed. Her state of mind was not helped when she arrived to at once sense an atmosphere of gloom. She was changing into her uniform when Simone came in and broke the news. Mrs Henderson had died in the night.

Anna was shattered. 'Died? But, Simone. . .' Fear that the nursing might have been at fault, that somehow she might have been responsible, gripped her. 'How? Her condition was serious but stable. . .why. . .?'

'Just one of those things, I suppose,' Simone said bleakly. 'She went into paradoxical breathing, and although they tried everything she didn't respond. Dr Carroll was here,' she added. 'She had the very best treatment. It wasn't anyone's fault.'

'No, of course not,' Anna said dully. But, as always when a patient died despite all the care the medical and nursing staff could give, she felt the burden of responsibility. Failure was hard to take.

There was no time, however, to brood, although Anna knew Mrs Henderson's death would needle her subconscious for a time. A new day brought a whole batch of new problems. What it did not bring was Dr Carroll. Anna guessed he might have taken the day off, seeing that he had apparently been at the hospital for most of the night. She guessed that he too was probably taking the loss of the patient hard. It should have been a relief not to have him interrupting, but, perversely, she missed him.

'Like a hole in the head,' she tried to tell herself once, then admitted that, whatever his faults, she was attracted to him, not just as a man with a powerful masculine attraction, but as a person. 'You have to be crazy,' she told herself.

It was only a day's respite. Dr Carroll was back on deck the following day. Having missed doing his usual round the previous day, he arrived bright and early, catching Anna and her staff slightly unprepared once again. Her conflicting feelings about him made her feel doubly on edge. She felt like a pressure cooker about to blow a valve.

Mrs Henderson's death had not helped. Everyone was still feeling touchy about it. Anna made only a brief remark to Scott, and, not unexpectedly, received only a monosyllabic acknowledgement. Clearly he did not wish to talk about it, so she judged it best not to try.

It had been altogether a very trying week, Anna admitted at the end of it. The previous weekend seemed light years ago and the slight temporary thawing of Dr Carroll a faint memory—or maybe something she had just imagined. Had she imagined the kiss too? If she had, it was a very vivid imagination she possessed! She could still feel the cool mist of droplets from the waterfall spray, the soft warmth of Scott's mouth on hers, the firm touch of his hands. . .

'Go away!' she commanded her thoughts. 'Go away and leave me alone. I can't stand the man!'

Later that day, she was in an empty ward with one of the other nurses trying to fix an intravenous drip stand which was faulty, when Dr Carroll walked in unannounced. Also in the recently vacated ward was Liz, who was removing a large bouquet of flowers which a patient who had just been discharged had not wanted to take with her, prior to remaking the bed.

She was heading for the door, holding the flowers in front of her, and they effectively hid Dr Carroll from her view, so as she approached the door and he burst through it, there was inevitably a collision.

Anna turned quickly as Liz let out a yelp of dismay, stumbled and then, realising whom she had bumped into, fled in terror, with Scott's exclamation, 'Stupid wench! Why don't you look where you're going?' echoing after her.

His words echoed for Anna too. He'd called her a stupid wench when he'd knocked her off her bicycle. What had Meg said about him? That he had a short fuse.

'Were you looking for me?' she asked, ignoring the outburst.

'Yes, I was.' He brushed petals and water splashes off his sleeve. 'Your wards are somewhat of a hazard, Sister Mackay!' Sometimes he relaxed and called her Anna, but not when he was cross!

'Oh, we've managed to avoid causing any casualties,' she replied, determined as usual not to let him rile her.

'More by luck than good management,' he suggested.

Anna ignored that remark too. 'You said you were looking for me?'

'Yes. Have you got the X-rays back yet for Gloria Trent?'

'That's the young woman with severe whiplash, isn't it?' Anna creased her brow. 'No, I'm sure we haven't. But if you come along to my office I'll check, and then if not I'll get on to Radiology. It was yesterday, wasn't it? So we should have had them by now.'

When confronted by his steely gaze, she always felt remiss, even if she had done nothing to warrant it. She preceded him to the door, but had scarcely reached it when there was an ominous sound behind her, a swish of footwear skidding on vinyl floor covering, accompanied by a grunt of surprise, and then a very clear expletive as the rear of Dr Carroll's anatomy hit the floor with a loud thud.

Anna found herself gazing down at his sprawled figure, feet slightly raised and a telltale squashed bloom on the sole of one shoe. She had missed stepping on the flower, but he had put his foot right on it and slipped as on a banana skin.

'Oh, dear!' she breathed, hurrying back to help him.

She bent over him. 'Are you hurt?' She held out a hand to help him up, but he ignored it.

He got to his feet, hair awry, face a little flushed, and said grittily, 'No, I'm not hurt, but I might have been.'

'You trod on a flower,' Anna said, and might have laughed because he looked so flustered, and no man liked a blow to his dignity, but she wasn't in the mood for laughing, not even at Scott Carroll.

He glowered at her. 'You'd better see it's cleaned up before someone does themselves a real injury. We've enough work to do in Theatre without in-house accidents to staff or patients.'

'Of course I'll do that straight away,' she said frostily. 'If you'd like to go to my office, I'll join you in a moment.'

No delay was necessary, however, as they met Liz in the corridor. This was unfortunate for the young nurse as she received a stinging reprimand, not the first she'd ever had, from Dr Carroll. Anna felt for her as she muttered apologies and then charged off to remove the squashed blooms and wipe the floor dry.

Now let him get cranky about the X-rays, thought Anna, and if he's not careful I'll clock him one!

She noticed, however, that the registrar looked a bit shaken, and her better nature won. 'Would you like a cup of tea?' she asked as he sat down rather gingerly in her visitor's chair. She added, 'You *have* hurt your back.'

'Just jarred it,' he said. 'It'll be all right in a minute. I wouldn't say no to the tea, thanks.'

Anna put her head out of the door and was lucky to catch Fran passing. 'Tea for two!' she whispered. 'Dr

Carroll tripped in Room Three and jarred his back. You'd better bring some codeine too.'

She wasn't sure, but she thought Fran's mouth moved in a silent 'Serves him right!'

When she returned to her desk, she noticed a large envelope there. It was from Radiology and must have arrived while she was attempting to repair the drip stand. 'I dare say this is what you're looking for,' she said, taking out the films. She noticed that when the registrar leaned forward to take them from her he winced.

She said, 'Don't you think you'd better have your back X-rayed? You might have done some real damage, chipped a bone or pulled a tendon.'

He grunted and studied the plates. 'Hmm. Looks like a compacted third vertebra.'

Fran came in with the tea and Anna shook a couple of codeine out of the bottle into the cap and handed them to Scott. 'Here, these'll ease the pain.'

He scowled, but took the tablets and downed them with the water Fran had thoughtfully provided. 'Thanks,' he said, then asked casually, 'Have you thought any more about taking up medicine again?'

His personal question came as a surprise. He hadn't talked to her about anything other than hospital matters all week. 'Not really. I'm still avoiding the issue, I'm afraid.'

'No point in leaving it too long,' he rejoined. 'The sooner you get started the better.'

He sat stiffly upright in the chair, which told Anna that his back really was hurting. He seemed in no hurry to move, however, but keen to discuss with her one or two patients who had had operations during the past couple of days. It was the first time, she realised, that he had ever sat down in her office. His comments and instructions were mostly given on the run, so to speak.

In spite of his brusqueness, it gave her a dangerous feeling of companionableness having him there drinking tea with her, and she found herself recalling that day they had gone bushwalking and to the pub afterwards. He had never suggested any further social contact and she believed he never would, but she wouldn't complain if he would do this more often—and if he would be a little less tetchy. There were times when he riled her, and other times, like this, when she felt she was catching a glimpse of the other side of the man, the side that was dangerously likeable. I wish I knew what bugs him, she thought.

The interlude was shortlived. Scott's pager broke into their conversation and he eased himself out of the chair to obey the summons. Anna could tell he was trying not to show that he was suffering any discomfort. He's probably only bruised his coccyx, she thought, but said nothing, because she knew he would not take advice from her.

That the incident with the flowers would have unexpected repercussions, Anna did not even consider. The next day the surgical registrar was obviously very stiff, although trying to disguise it.

'He ought to get his back X-rayed,' Simone observed.

Anna shrugged. 'So I told him, but you know what doctors are. Maybe we should have a word with one of the others and get them to persuade him. Or maybe Matron could.'

'Or we let him stew in his own juice,' said Simone with humour rather than malice.

By the end of that Friday afternoon, Anna was almost at the end of her tether. It had been a frantic week and she was longing to get home, have a nice hot scented bath, and go to bed. Maybe next week would be better.

She was just clearing up some paperwork in her office prior to handing over to the incoming nurse when there was a rap at her door. She looked up to find that her visitor was young Liz Farmer. That wasn't unusual, but what was was that the girl's eyes were puffy and red, although she had tried to disguise it with make-up. She had obviously been crying.

'Liz, what's the matter?' Anna forgot her weariness for a moment in her concern for the young nurse who worried her quite a bit anyway.

'C-can I talk to you for a minute?' Liz asked hesitantly. 'I—I know you're about to go off, but. . .'

'Is it important?' asked Anna, sensing it must be.

Liz nodded. 'Yes, it is. . .but if you. . .'

'Sit down, Liz. You'd better tell me about it.' Anna waved her into a chair and looked anxiously across the desk at the girl. The large blue eyes were about to brim with tears, she suspected. 'Now, what's the problem?'

Liz was screwing a handkerchief into a tight ball in her fists. She looked down into her lap for a moment, then took a deep breath. 'I—I want to leave. . .'

Anna was shaken. 'Leave, Liz? You mean work in another hospital?'

The girl shook her head. 'No. No, I want to leave nursing. I—I don't think I'm cut out for it, Anna. I'm too stupid and clumsy, and——'

'Hey, just a minute!' Shocked, Anna rose and went around the desk to confront her at close quarters. 'Liz, listen to me. Just because you make a few mistakes, drop a few things, that doesn't mean you're not cut out to be a nurse. A little more experience and you'll be fine.'

But Liz was determined. 'I don't think so. I've been thinking it over, and after—after Dr Carroll tripped up yesterday because I wasn't looking where I was going and I dropped some flowers and didn't notice—I mean, I should have, shouldn't I? I should have wiped up the water straight away, but I didn't think. . . I only thought about getting out of there and away from——' She broke off and clamped her lips tightly together.

'He intimidates you, doesn't he?' said Anna, feeling a wave of anger, both at Scott for his insensitivity and Liz for her over-sensitiveness. She went on, 'I'm afraid you're likely to meet quite a few people like that, Liz, people who are always finding fault with you, but it doesn't mean you're stupid or not cut out to be a nurse. You just have to learn to take it in your stride.'

'As you do,' said Liz, smiling a little.

'Look, Dr Carroll drives me mad at times too,' Anna admitted. 'But mostly he's right, you know. It's just that he's a bit curt sometimes, maybe not as easygoing as some doctors.'

Liz looked very wan. 'I can't sleep for worrying about it,' she confessed. 'I know I'm not going to be any good. I'm afraid I might do something really terrible one day. I think I'd better give it up now before I do. I know he thinks I'm hopeless, and I suppose you all do too.'

Anna bit her lip. 'You like nursing, though?'

Liz swallowed and nodded. 'Yes. . . I always wanted to look after sick people, but it's no good if you're the wrong sort, and I am.'

Anna didn't know what to do. Liz had obviously thought it over very thoroughly. What made her mad, though, was that it was Scott Carroll's fault. He'd undermined the girl's confidence. No, perhaps they had all done that to an extent, but he had sent her over the top. He'd reduced her to a bundle of nerves every time she encountered him. Anna considered the girl for a moment or two.

Eventually she said, 'Look, Liz, don't do anything rash. If it's Dr Carroll who's getting under your skin, maybe you can transfer to another ward—Medical or Children's. Would you like me to have a word with Matron?'

But Liz was adamant. 'No, it's no good, Anna. My mind's made up. I really don't think I should stay in nursing.'

Anna moistened her lips anxiously. 'Very well, Liz, but I think you're making a mistake. You're giving in too soon. Wasting all that training. All you need is a bit more experience.'

Liz shook her head. She was more in control of herself now. 'I know you're trying to be kind, but it's no use.'

Anna's phone rang, and Liz slipped out of the office. Anna turned to face out of her window as she talked to the mother of the teenager who had had her appendix out the previous day. The mountains were clearly etched against the sky and clouds were piled up behind them. While she talked, her mind was in turmoil, her feelings churning because of Liz's visit. And most of what she was feeling was anger towards Scott Carroll. When she put the phone down and turned, she was shocked to see him in the doorway.

She stared at him. She felt a mixture of extreme

tiredness and unleashed fury. She felt something inside her snap and catapult her over the top. She had never believed that people actually did see red, but at that moment she did. Before he had a chance to say what he wanted, she let fly.

'Dr Carroll, just the person I wanted to see! Do come in!'

He looked mildly taken aback at her belligerent tone, but moved into the office and shut the door. 'You seem upset about something,' he observed.

'Upset? I'm livid! I've just had a junior nurse in here wanting to resign—and it's all your fault!'

'My fault?'

'Yes. In fact I'm surprised, Dr Carroll, that half the nursing staff in the MWH haven't resigned, those on our surgical wards, anyway.'

'What in heaven's name are you talking about?' He sounded annoyed now.

'I'm talking about your abrasiveness, Dr Carroll. The way you ride roughshod over everybody, call young nurses "stupid wench" and older ones too on occasions! I'm talking about your constant fault-finding, nit-picking, thoroughly aggravating attitude. I've just had a girl in here whose self-esteem is at an all-time low because you made her feel that way. Every time you appear she goes to pieces. She's going to give up nursing because you've made her feel she's hopeless. You're the most insensitive, arrogant boor I've ever come across!'

Dr Carroll stared at her as though she had gone mad. 'How dare you speak to me like that?' he said in a chilly tone, and turned and slammed out of her office.

Anna sank into the chair Liz had vacated only

minutes ago, her head in her hands. 'Oh, God,' she moaned. 'What have I done?'

She looked up at the closed door on which there still seemed to be an imprint of Dr Carroll's outraged face. 'Oh, Liz,' she whispered, 'I'll have to resign too now.'

CHAPTER SIX

THERE was nothing like a hot, scented bath to soothe away tiredness in the limbs and tension in the mind, Anna thought as she luxuriated in the tub that evening.

'What a week!' she murmured aloud as she huddled under the perfumed foam and let the warmth pervade her whole body. It was hardly any wonder it had ended the way it had. Poor Liz, she thought, but not poor Anna. She would have to resign, of course. It would be impossible to work with Scott now that she had yelled at him in such an insulting way. Maybe she should try and contact Matron over the weekend and make a clean breast of it. Doubtless Matron would say it would be better if Anna didn't even go back on Monday. An ignominious departure, but at that moment Anna would have welcomed that suggestion.

'What a mess!' she sighed regretfully. 'Why didn't I keep my temper and just ask him to be a little more considerate? I might even have persuaded Liz not to quit, but I fluffed it. . .' She felt disgusted with herself. It was ironic that she had been the one who had proved to have a short fuse. She could still see Scott Carroll's outraged expression as he'd slammed out of her office, and it filled her with a strange mixture of fury and sadness.

When the water cooled, she pulled the plug and stepped out of the bath, wrapping herself in a warm towel and vigorously drying her skin, which glowed from the immersion in hot water. She flung on a dark blue velour dressing-gown and matching slippers, and screwed her hair, which she had put up while in the bath, into a tighter knot, but damp tendrils still clung to her temples and neck. She was tempted to go straight to bed and let all her problems wait until tomorrow, but she hankered for a cup of coffee and supposed she ought to try and eat something. She'd had nothing much for lunch again today. It was easier to believe that the hollow feeling inside her was due only to hunger.

She was making toasted sandwiches when the door-bell rang. A little warily, she went into the hall and called out, 'Who is it?'

The last person she expected answered, 'Scott Carroll.'

Anna felt the blood drain from her cheeks. What on earth was he doing here? She gave her slightly dishevelled appearance a frantic glance, then opened the door. He didn't give her a chance to speak, but said quickly, 'I think we need to talk.'

'Do we?' She just stared at him.

'We do,' he insisted, adding pointedly, 'It will be a little chilly standing on the doorstep.'

Anna felt weak at the knees. 'Yes, I suppose so.'

He stepped into the hall and she closed the door. When she turned, his gaze flicked over her. 'I'm sorry for interrupting—you were. . .' he smiled in an awkward kind of way '. . .washing your hair?'

'I just had a bath,' said Anna, unable to get any kind of expression into her voice. She ran her hands nervously down her dressing-gown. 'Sorry I'm not dressed. . . I wasn't expecting. . .company. I was going to have an early night.'

The dark eyebrows slid together. 'It's been a bad week?'

'Hectic,' she admitted. Then, shrugging, 'But it often is. That's nursing. I'm sure you find surgery even more taxing.'

His eyes narrowed. 'You don't have to belittle what you do.'

Anna stiffened. 'I wasn't. I have total respect for my profession.' Did he think she despised nursing because she'd wanted to be a doctor? The implication hurt, which made her angry again.

He clapped a hand to his forehead. 'God, you're touchy today. I didn't mean. . .' He looked at her despairingly. 'I guess I shouldn't have come. I should have given you time to calm down.'

Anna bit her lip. She wished he hadn't, and yet a part of her she didn't understand was glad to see him. But what was the point of their talking? Did he hope to persuade her to apologise? Well, she would do so if it would do any good, but she was afraid it wouldn't. They would clash again. It would be better if she resigned. She said, 'You'd better come and sit down.' She led him into the living-room, and as she did so, the smell of burning hit her nostrils. 'Oh, hell, my sandwiches!'

She ran out to the kitchen, muttering crossly as she extricated her burnt offering from under the grill and tipped it into the garbage bucket. When she looked round, Scott was lounging in the doorway.

'Sorry I distracted you,' he said.

His mild manner disconcerted her. 'Doesn't matter, I can make some more,' she answered, then paused expectantly. Whatever he had to say, let him say it here now and go. He was making her feel edgy. And then she heard herself saying, 'Have you had a meal? I'll make you some too if you like.'

His astonishment was only momentary. 'That's very kind. I haven't eaten, as a matter of fact. I wanted to talk to you as soon as I could.'

Anna avoided his gaze. 'I guess I owe you an apology,' she said, getting in first. 'I went a bit over the top. It was just that Liz wanting to resign was the last straw, and when you came in. . .' She slid the new batch of sandwiches under the grill and set about making another couple of rounds. 'In the circumstances I've decided I must resign myself. I'll see Matron on Monday.' She tried to sound matter-of-fact, to conceal the raw emotion she felt.

Scott reacted unexpectedly. 'Not on my account you won't!' He marched across the kitchen and grabbed her by the shoulders. There was outrage of a different kind in his eyes now. 'Don't be bloody stupid! There's no earthly reason why you should resign. *I* behaved abominably. And I'm here now to apologise.'

His grey eyes bored into hers until she felt her insides melting, all her resolution blown to bits. She could only give a rueful smile. 'You had reason enough to slam out.' She jerked away from him to rescue the sandwiches.

'Not if what you said was true.' He pulled out a chair from the kitchen table and sank into it.

He was as weary as she, Anna thought. They'd both been at flash point. She caught his eye again and saw anguish in the grey depths. She had wounded the man, she realised, with sudden sharp regret. 'Liz is very sensitive,' she said slowly. 'She takes things to heart. She was very upset, but I suppose I can try again to talk her out of resigning.'

Scott looked at her for a long moment. Then quietly he said, 'No, I'll talk to her.'

Anna's mouth dropped open, but she said nothing. The thought of Dr Carroll trying to persuade Liz not to give up nursing was a feat for the imagination, and almost made her smile. But if he actually did. . . She looked at him in wonderment. Humility didn't come easily to anyone, and she admired him for what he'd said.

She said simply, 'Thank you, Scott. I think that would restore her confidence. She's not really a bad nurse, just lacking self-esteem.'

'I know. . .'

Anna used the egg slice to transfer a round of perfect golden toasted sandwiches on to a plate which she pushed across the table to him. 'Coffee?' she asked, and he nodded, then said,

'I don't suppose you've got anything stronger first up?'

'Wine? There's a cask of dry red.'

'I think that would go admirably with the feast,' he said, and she felt herself relaxing. This was the Scott Carroll she'd walked in the bush with, had tea with at the Winston pub, the Scott who sometimes had a glint of humour in his eyes, and who had impulsively kissed her. . .

She fetched wine glasses and paper napkins and joined him at the kitchen table, while still keeping an eye on the grill. Scott filled their glasses from the cask. He held his towards her.

'Cheers.'

'Cheers,' she replied, feeling a slow warmth stealing over her.

They ate in silence. After the sandwiches, Anna

offered fruit, and finally the coffee which had been keeping hot on its own hotplate.

Scott stirred a spoonful of sugar into his, then lifted his gaze to Anna and said in a tone of real dismay, 'Have I really been so unbearable? A boor, an insensitive wretch, a bad-tempered. . .?' He stopped, looking more stricken than she would have thought possible. 'I wasn't aware. . .'

Anna said quietly, 'Perhaps you had a reason. Sometimes people don't realise they're taking out their own personal problems on others.' She paused, giving him the opportunity to deny it.

He looked startled, then gave a lopsided grin. 'Maybe you ought to become a psychiatrist!'

She blushed. 'Sorry.'

There was a lengthy silence and Anna was sure she had offended him by her oblique prying, but suddenly he said, 'You're right, you know. That's probably what I have been doing, not deliberately, but unconsciously.' He brushed his hair back with both hands, in agitation, then gave her a long considering look. 'I might as well tell you, I suppose. You're not the kind who gossips. I'm not making excuses, and I'm not looking for sympathy—but I do have a big problem in my life. . .'

'You don't have to tell me about it,' she said hurriedly. 'It's enough to. . .'

He smiled at her wryly. 'Maybe I need to talk about it. Maybe bottling it all up has been half the problem. My problem, Anna, is—my wife.'

She drew a sharp breath and a feeling of intense disappointment flooded over her. He was married. Well, she ought not to be surprised at that, a good-looking man of his age.

'Scott, are you sure you want to tell me about her?' she asked, not sure she wanted to hear after all.

He ignored that protest too. 'There isn't much to tell,' he said. 'Janis and I married five years ago, and we've been living apart for the past two. At first I thought separation would ultimately lead to reconciliation, but it didn't. She's divorcing me—with my consent. It was a strange feeling when she told me. I experienced the most overwhelming sense of—of void. It was. . .' He raked his hair again, unable to find adequate words to explain.

Anna suggested softly, 'A sense of failure?'

He nodded bleakly. 'Yes, exactly that. And a blow to my ego too, I suppose. I felt cast off, unwanted, like something that hasn't come up to expectations and has been discarded.'

'Is she marrying someone else?' she queried.

'No.' He laughed harshly. 'No, she's married to her career. She's a gynaecologist, with sky's-the-limit ambitions. She has a chance to go overseas and thinks it might be better if she's totally free.'

'Do you still love her?' she dared to ask.

He looked startled at the question, was silent for a moment, then said, 'No, I don't think so. How can you still love someone who's drained you dry of everything you can offer and then abandoned you?'

Anna smiled. 'People are quite extraordinary sometimes where emotions are concerned.'

'I admire her,' he admitted reluctantly. 'She's never let anything stand in her way. Being a woman has never been an obstacle to Janis. She married me, I suspect, because it brought her in touch with people she thought might help her career, which it did, and I didn't mind that. . .' He banged his palms helplessly on the table. 'But now she doesn't have any more use for me. . .'

'That's pretty hard to take,' said Anna. 'I'm not surprised you feel used, and frustrated and at odds with the world.'

'I'm saying it's Janis's fault, that she made me mean,' he said, 'and that's not fair really—to blame her. It's not all her fault that our marriage was a failure. I should have had more sense, I should have been more aware of the kind of person I was marrying, but I fell for her, her looks, her strong personality, her. . .'

'Sexuality,' said Anna, a little shocked at her daring.

Scott looked a shade embarrassed. 'All right, yes. She was good in bed. . .' He turned his palms upwards. 'Relationships based only on sex seldom last. I've only got myself to blame.'

'And you blame yourself too much,' Anna said. 'When you're lashing out at other people you're really lashing out at yourself. And at Janis too. You can't hurt her, so you hurt others.'

'You put it in a nutshell. Not a very nice picture, is it?'

'It's pretty normal,' she said encouragingly. 'You'll probably see things differently once your divorce is through. At the moment you're probably subconsciously still hoping for a miracle, that maybe she'll change her mind, want a reconciliation after all.'

'It wouldn't work,' Scott said gloomily. 'I realise that now.'

'No, but it would restore your self-esteem, put you back in charge, reverse that terrible sense of failure you're suffering.'

He looked at her musingly. 'You're probably right. But there's no chance she'll want me back. None at all.' He balled a fist and slammed it into his other hand. 'Anna, thank you for listening to me. And thank you for trying to help. I'm sorry I barged in on you when you meant to have an early night, but I couldn't let things stand as they were. You gave me one hell of a jolt, which I needed. I hope I won't give you cause to read the riot act to me again!' He paused, smiling. 'You won't resign?'

'No—not yet, anyway.'

'Not until you decide to take up medicine again?'

'If I do. . .'

Scott rose hurriedly and then involuntarily sagged, his hand on the small of his back as a short sharp grunt of pain escaped him.

'Your back!' exclaimed Anna, getting up too. 'You really ought to let someone look at it.'

He grimaced and slowly straightened up. 'I did. I had an X-ray just before I came to your office and you flew at me.'

'What did you come for?' she asked.

'Oh, just to have a look at some case-notes, nothing urgent,' he said dismissively.

'And the X-ray. Did you get the result?'

'Yes. Nothing chipped or cracked or damaged. Just a strain.' He rummaged in his pocket. 'Pharmacy gave me this and said to rub it in before I went to bed.' He tossed the tube of deep heat treatment on the table.

'That should help,' she agreed, reading the label.

'It'd better. I've got a big list tomorrow.'

'Yes, you have,' she murmured, remembering. 'But they're mostly elective, aren't they? They can be put off if necessary.'

'I hate putting people off,' said Scott. 'It's a real let-down once they've psyched themselves up to have the op. Then they've got to go through it all again.' He moved gingerly. 'Well, I'd better be going. Let you get to bed.'

Anna accompanied him to the front door, but was concerned at the stiff way he walked, as though his back was causing considerable pain. He glanced at her. 'I seem to have seized up.'

'Well, don't forget to use that rub,' she reminded him.

'Yes, Sister—I mean, no, Sister!'

The look on his face was one of stoic endurance. Anna didn't know whether he lived alone or not, so she said, 'I hope there's someone who can rub your back for you? You can't really massage it properly yourself.'

'No, there isn't. I live alone,' he said. 'But don't worry, I'll manage.'

She heard herself saying impulsively, 'I'll rub it for you if you like.'

'No. . .really. . .'

'Come on, it won't take long. Give me that tube.'

He looked taken aback, and she laughed. 'What's the matter? I'm a nurse. You'd let Marie do it, wouldn't you?'

A defensive look came into his eyes. 'She's a physiotherapist.'

'And I'm not. I'm not going to try and give you a full-scale massage, Dr Carroll, just a rub,' Anna said, amused now. 'I'm quite competent to do that. You needn't strip off! If you just come into the living-room, loosen your trousers a little and pull up your sweater, I'll be able to hit the spot quite easily.'

He hobbled into the living-room and, as Anna then suggested, leaned forward over the back of an armchair instead of lying down. She warmed her hands in front of the fire, then uncapped the tube and squeezed some of the pinkish cream on to her fingertips. A strong eucalyptus vapour made her nostrils tingle.

'Smells like powerful stuff,' Scott said, pulling his sweater up and yanking his shirt out of his trousers to reveal an expanse of tanned muscular back. He loosened his strides and eased them down his hips a little. Anna noticed a rim of dark blue briefs.

She placed a hand on the small of his back in the right lumbar region. 'Now tell me where it hurts most.' She began slow circular movements, spreading the cream across his lower back.

'Bit to the left,' he said. 'Yes, more on the left side. Mmm, that's it. . .ah. . .yes. . .*ouch*!'

'Sorry!' Anna gently massaged the cream in. Although his skin and her hands were warm, it took quite a time to disappear.

'Mmm, that's the spot,' Scott murmured once or twice. 'Maybe you should take up physiotherapy.'

'It's too much like hard work,' she said. 'You need stamina for that job. But I've had quite a bit of experience of this. My mother had a bad back.' She was beginning to wish she had not offered to rub the doctor's. There was something a little too intimate about it, and her initial clinical detachment was becoming overlaid by a distinctly pleasurable sensation, a desire to caress rather than rub. At last the cream disappeared, leaving a reddened patch.

'There you are—done,' said Anna, taking her hand away. 'That should ease it a bit.'

Scott turned round without effort. 'Mmm, feels better already.' He was smiling in a way she had never seen before, and it made the colour surge into her face.

'You'd better see Marie tomorrow,' Anna advised. 'She'll give you a real massage.'

'I think the present one was quite satisfactory,' Scott said, and the direction of his gaze drew her horrified attention to the fact that the exertion of rubbing his back had caused her dressing-gown cord to slacken and that now the crossover revealed rather more of the swell of her breasts than she felt comfortable about.

With her hands still sticky with the rub, she was reluctant to adjust her dressing-gown. Hands flapping, she said as composedly as possible, 'I'd better wash my hands. Can you let yourself out?'

Scott looked at her for a moment, then deftly gathered her in a tight embrace. His mouth devoured hers with a desperate hunger, more passionately than that day by the waterfall, and Anna felt her whole body go slack. He held her fiercely and she felt the fire burning in him begin to consume her also. No one, she realised in panic, had ever stirred her senses quite like this.

'Anna. . .' Scott lifted his lips from hers, and there was a wild kind of light in his grey eyes which might have been the reflection of the fire or something more dangerous. 'Anna, do you have any idea how beautiful you are?' His hands brushed roughly up her arms, gripping her shoulders, and she was drawn hard against him as he leaned on the back of the chair, all back pain forgotten. He took a strand of her hair and curled it around one finger, smiling as though a little bemused. Then he reached into the pile of hair behind her head and released it from the combs she had used to pin it up while she had her bath. The dark waves cascaded down over her shoulders and he ran his fingers through the silky tresses with obvious enjoyment.

'You're a very tantalising woman,' he murmured, and bent his head to kiss the curve of her shoulder, trailing his mouth nimbly across her collarbone, and before she realised his intention his hands had pushed aside the loosened gown and exposed one breast. Seeing the hardened nipple which she was powerless to control, he lowered his mouth to taste the rosy tip, and she shuddered with an exquisite pleasure.

Realising now that she was in fact naked under the dressing-gown, he took full advantage of the fact and sensuously caressed her thigh while drawing her closer and claiming her mouth once more. Mesmerised by the heightening of her own as well as his desire, Anna was unable to prevent her own responses, which encouraged him all the more. Never in her life before had such delicious sensations overwhelmed her body.

At last Scott broke the kiss and smiled at her smoulderingly. 'Maybe it's just as well you don't intend taking up physio. . .your massaging is a mite too inflammatory!'

Anna had never felt so confused. She burbled idiotically, 'I must wash this stuff off my hands.'

He chuckled, drawing her back between his thighs. 'I don't know what you've done to me, Anna, but I haven't let go like this in a long time. . .'

'Neither have I!' she exclaimed, hands still flapping stupidly because although she ached to touch him, she didn't want to put grease on his clothes.

'All the time you were rubbing my back it was agony,' he confessed.

'I thought it was helping.'

'The backache, yes, but you have the kind of hands that are very arousing, Anna. I was burning to touch you too. . .'

'You seem to have succeeded somewhat,' she said in a dry tone. She tried to pull away. 'I think this has gone far enough, Dr Carroll. Please let me go. I think we both got a bit carried away.'

'Of course we did. Why not? I'm very attracted to you, Anna. I found you quite irresistible the day I knocked you off your bicycle and for one ghastly moment I thought I'd killed you. All those damn freesias scattered over you, like a funeral. . .'

She could not help a chuckle. 'You called me a stupid wench.'

'I know. You had to be, or else it was all my fault. . .which it was. I was going too fast.' He cupped her face in his hands and kissed her lips. 'Let's make love, Anna,' he whispered softly. 'I want you so much. . .'

And I want you, Anna thought, her need a desperate ache. For a moment she forgot her hands were still sticky with the rub and let them touch his hair, stray down his backbone, then as the fires within responded, she struggled to free herself again.

'No, Scott. . .' And she was saying, fatuously, 'My hands are all sticky.'

He tightened his grip on her waist. 'If I let you go and wash them, you won't come back, will you?'

Caught out, she shook her head. 'Scott, I do find you very attractive, but I don't think. . .well, I—don't go to bed with someone just because he. . .' She didn't know how to make her refusal sound rational.

He released her abruptly. 'No, of course not. Perhaps it was rather impetuous of me.' He gave her a long look that almost catapulted her back into his arms. Then he laughed. 'I dare say, in view of the state of my back, also somewhat foolish! Not to mention ambitious.' He caught her in his arms again, but lightly now. 'Thank you, Anna. You did me the world of good tonight. And I don't just mean the back rub. You eased a lot of other pain as well.' He pushed her gently away. 'Now go and wash that stuff off your hands, and go to bed. And don't worry about Liz—I'll talk to her.'

He tucked in his shirt and buckled his belt, pulled his sweater down over it, and made for the front door. Anna muttered a feeble goodnight, and when he had gone she stood for a long time in the dark hallway, her eyes filled with tears.

CHAPTER SEVEN

'I DON'T know why everyone laughs,' complained Margery Watts, a new patient in the women's surgical ward. 'A bunion is a very painful condition.' She smiled goodhumouredly none the less as she accepted the pre-medication Fran was offering her.

'We're not laughing,' said Fran, straight-faced, 'are we, Anna?'

'Definitely not,' agreed Anna, her mouth crinkling at the corners. She was checking on the patients due for operations that morning. Mrs Watts was first on the list. She said, 'I think it must have been that old music-hall song in which the woman sings about raising a bunion on his Spanish onion, if she catches her man bending. I'm afraid it always strikes me as anatomically a bit odd.'

'Can you have a bunion on the coccyx?' asked Fran, and Anna shrugged her doubt.

Margery laughed. 'My mother used to love those old music-hall songs. We used to sing around the piano when I was a girl.' She sighed nostalgically, 'And we went to dances every Saturday night. We didn't have television, of course, but we didn't miss it!'

'And by the time you were into high heels, pointy toes were in fashion,' Anna said. 'Dancing in tight shoes was probably the start of your trouble.'

The patient agreed. 'When you've got largish feet, like me, you do tend to try and cram them into shoes that are too small. Oh, I remember agonies, dancing in

110

tight shoes! In the hot weather, my feet would swell. . .' She winced with the recollection.

'Well, if you take good care after the operation, you should have no more problems with this foot,' Anna told her. 'And the other one isn't so bad. You mightn't need an op on that one, I think Dr Carroll said.'

Margery was already relaxing as intended. She nodded and smiled dreamily. 'Dr Carroll's a lovely man, isn't he?'

'A very good surgeon,' Anna agreed, not to be drawn into giving an opinion on his personality.

But Fran said, 'He's not always as sweet-tempered with the staff as he is with the patients, Margery.'

Margery sighed. 'It probably depends who he's sweet on! Maybe he doesn't want to give you girls any wrong ideas. He's not the sort of man to philander, I'd say.'

Fran snorted, 'You can say that again!' She added, 'We'll be back for you shortly. You're lucky being first. It'll all be over and done with by morning teatime!'

A short time later, back in her office for a few moments, Anna paused and gazed out of the window at the mountains. She was still wondering anxiously how Scott was this morning, but there had been no direct word from him. It would not be surprising if he avoided her, she realised. She wasn't sure how she would cope with a confrontation after all that had happened on Friday. Especially on Friday evening. . .

Her skin tingled at the memory, as it had done all weekend whenever she thought of Scott Carroll's kiss, his sensuous caressing, and the extraordinary pleasure she had experienced in his arms. It was crazy. One minute on Friday afternoon she had been yelling at him, and only hours later she had been in his arms. One minute she'd been furious with him, then the next rubbing his injured back. Thinking about what he had told her, and how she had reacted to him, made her go hot and cold by turns, and however she tried to rationalise it her emotions still ended up in confusion.

How was he feeling? she wondered. Probably he was regretting the impulse that had made him react so strongly to her. And what about Liz? That problem still hovered around the edge of Anna's thoughts. Liz was on duty this shift, but apart from a brief greeting Anna had had no conversation with her. The ward was extra busy, with several patients going to Theatre that morning, and Anna knew she would not have a chance to speak to her until later in the day, and she wasn't sure what she would say when the opportunity did occur. Would Scott talk to her as he'd promised? Anna felt doubtful. On reflection, he might decide he'd been rather rash and change his mind about that.

Anna was having a cup of coffee mid-morning when Marie, the physiotherapist, looked in on her way to attending to several patients who needed her attention.

'Hi, Anna.' She folded her arms across her chest and with mock severity demanded, 'What have you lot been doing to Dr Carroll?'

The question was so unexpected, Anna felt her cheeks warm. 'Doing?' she queried.

'He tripped on spilt flowers, so he told me,' said Marie, her face breaking into a grin. 'On *your* ward. He came along for a ten-minute massage before operating this morning. I told him he shouldn't be operating, but he insisted. No doubt he'll stiffen up and need another session afterwards.'

'His back's still painful?' asked Anna, all too vividly reminded of her own efforts at massaging Scott's back, and wondering if he would have told Marie about it.

No, she reflected, it was unlikely he would have done that.

'Yes, but there's no real damage—he had it X-rayed. So you can breathe again—he won't be suing!'

'Do you think he ought to be operating?' Anna queried.

'Oh, he'll be OK so long as he takes a couple of suitable strong painkillers and doesn't bend or reach too far too suddenly,' said Marie confidently. She laughed. 'I dare say the smell of liniment will gag the rest of his team, though! And he's bound to get a few ribald remarks thrown at him by one of our smart-Aleck interns.'

Anna felt her cheeks warming again. Nobody knew that Scott Carroll had been at her place on Friday night, nobody knew that such ribald remarks might just have had some substance if Scott hadn't already ricked his back.

'Well, I hope he doesn't get any violent twinges,' she said. 'It could be dangerous—to the patient, I mean.'

Marie was still amused by the situation. 'And the staff! You know how tetchy he can be at times, and lumbago is not a complaint to put one in a good mood.' She added seriously, 'But I don't think Dr Carroll would ever do anything that might endanger a patient. If he didn't think he was capable of operating today, he wouldn't do it. I've no worries, Anna. He'll just be a bit stiff later, that's all. Be nice to him! If you don't want a ton of bricks to fall, humour the man.'

'We do!' returned Anna, smiling as though it were a joke. Would Scott be any different, she wondered, since their talk on Friday? Would her yelling at him really make any difference?

Marie breezed off to her patients, and Anna thoughtfully contemplated the white wall of her office. But there was no time for lengthy contemplation; there was too much to do with patients returning to the ward from the theatre, and that afternoon they would be admitting two new ones. She went to find Fran, whose quiet competence kept the ward running smoothly whatever the crises.

Anna had just supervised the return to the ward of the last patient on the operating list, yet another appendicectomy, and was thinking about snatching some lunch, when Liz approached her rather diffidently.

'Anna, can you spare a minute?'

Anna nodded and ushered Liz into her office, preparing herself to take up where they'd left off on Friday. She was determined to try and persuade Liz to change her mind, but she couldn't say that Scott would speak to her in case he'd changed his mind about that. So how could she convince Liz that things would be different? She wasn't at all sure herself that they would be.

Liz shook her head when invited to sit down. 'It won't take a minute,' she said. 'I just wanted to tell you I've changed my mind, and I'm sorry I went off the handle a bit last Friday. . .'

Anna felt a huge sigh of relief escape her. She smiled broadly. 'Liz, I'm so glad. . . I was afraid you were going to act hastily. . .but you thought it over at the weekend, did you?'

'No, I didn't,' Liz confessed. 'My mind was quite made up. I was going to tell you today and ask how I went about resigning, but. . .'

Anna's eyes were widening. 'But what?'

Liz screwed her face up and looked embarrassed.

'Dr Carroll sent for me a few minutes ago and he—he talked me out of it.' She looked astonished.

'Did he indeed?' Anna pretended not to have any prior knowledge of his intention. 'And how did he manage that?'

'He said you'd told him I was planning to give up nursing, and he said it was a terrible waste of all that training if I did. He was so *nice*, Anna. . .' Liz chuckled. 'He even said he was sorry if he was sometimes a bit grumpy and bowled people out, but that doctors and nurses were all humans too and had to learn to be tolerant of each other, and considerate. He said he knew he wasn't always as considerate as he might be, but he believed in the highest of standards for himself and everyone else and was very impatient with sloppiness. He sort of apologised for being efficient!'

'I can see you were charmed,' Anna remarked.

Liz spread her hands. 'How could I help it? He was so different, and he made me feel so much better about everything. He said I mustn't give up just because I felt everyone was picking on me, but to try and learn from my mistakes. He said he thought most of it was probably only in my mind anyway, because from what he'd heard I was getting on all right. . .' She looked anxiously at Anna.

'Of course you are,' said Anna. 'And he's right— we've all been through similar bad patches. It comes from being conscientious, which isn't a bad fault.' She smiled encouragingly. 'Another six months and you'll wonder what you were worrying about. So, no more talk about resigning?'

'I couldn't now, could I?' said Liz. 'Not after Dr Carroll's been so kind. . .' She faltered, 'I—I don't feel quite so intimidated by him now. Underneath he's really quite nice, isn't he?'

'Yes, I think he is,' agreed Anna. She added with another smile, 'And I think you really do like nursing, don't you, Liz?'

The young nurse answered softly, 'Yes, I do. Very much.'

'And that's what counts. Enthusiasm and dedication, and a strong sense of your responsibilities. I think you'll make a very good nurse, Liz. If you find things getting you down, don't be afraid to come and have a chat so we can sort things out before they get too desperate.'

'That's what Dr Carroll said I must do,' said Liz, wide-eyed. 'He said you were the kind of person who could solve most problems.'

'Did he?' Anna felt a warm glow at the reported compliment, but was unwilling to agree with it. 'Well, I think he's a bit off the mark there, but it's always worth talking over a problem, I think. Sometimes it just helps you to work out the solution for yourself.'

When Liz had gone, Anna breathed a silent thank-you to Scott Carroll. It couldn't have been easy to apologise to a junior nurse, but he'd done it, and she admired him for that. Now, she reflected in amusement, he had probably gained a devoted slave for life—as well as a good many more points on her table of estimation. Not the least of them was for keeping to his operating schedule today despite back pain. And he'd managed to find the time to keep his promise to talk to Liz as well.

Knowing that Scott would eventually come to see the patients he had operated on that morning, Anna found herself in a state of mixed dread and anticipation as she faced the afternoon. Every glimpse of a white coat, a dark head, made her heart pound, but it was when she was least expecting him that Scott finally visited the ward.

Anna had been having a reassuring chat to a new patient who had been admitted for surgery for a particularly severe hiatus hernia. She had told the patient that the surgeon and the anaesthetist would explain exactly what was going to happen, and that the slight discomfort she would experience after the operation would only be very temporary.

'We'll have your chest X-rayed the day after surgery,' Anna told her, 'and if everything is OK Dr Carroll will remove the drain which he will have inserted to carry away any blood or secretions. We'll keep you in for a few days just to make sure you're healing properly, but recovery after this operation is usually very fast, with no problems.'

'I still don't like the idea of it,' insisted the middle-aged woman. 'I've never been in hospital in my life before.'

Anna said consolingly, 'Then just think of it as an interesting experience.'

As she stepped outside the room into the corridor and was about to cross it to her office, Scott Carroll burst through the double doors behind her.

'Anna!'

Her thoughts had for once been miles away from him and the sound of his voice sent fiery shocks through her. She turned round. 'Oh, hello. . .' She was sure her face was scarlet, and certainly her knees were trembling. She felt as tongue-tied as a first-year student in the presence of a professor, and just stood there staring at him. He seemed equally interested in appraising her.

Finally he said, 'Everything OK?'

Anna came to her senses. 'If you mean the patients who had surgery this morning, yes. You've come to see them?' Fatuous question, of course he had.

'And you. . .' he murmured, with the kind of look she would have preferred not to have to cope with on duty.

'How's your back?' she asked, walking briskly towards the ward where most of the post-operative patients were. 'I hear you had to have physiotherapy this morning to make you fit to operate.'

He let his hand rest on her shoulder. 'Yes. It works for surgeons just as much as for footballers. Mind you, I felt pretty stiff after eight ops—still do. I have to be careful not to bend too low.'

Anna paused at the ward door. 'Liz told me you'd spoken to her. I want to thank you. . .'

He shrugged. 'I suppose she'll tell the whole hospital.'

'I doubt it. Liz is a quiet one, and doesn't gossip. I don't think she'd want to talk about wanting to resign.'

The door opened and Fran almost walked into them, bearing a bedpan.

'Oops, sorry,' she said, giving Scott an uncertain glance as though she expected him to say something.

Dr Carroll frowned but said nothing. He and Anna went into the ward, and Fran, joining Liz in the sluice, said, 'Do you know, I've got a feeling that Dr Carroll has taken a fancy to our Anna Mackay, and that maybe it's mutual.'

Liz's eyes widened. 'Really? Why?'

'They were lurking together outside the door of

Room Four, and she was decidedly pink! And I've never seen him looking as though butter wouldn't melt in his mouth before. Maybe that's all he needs—a good woman to thaw him out!'

Liz smiled to herself. Maybe the thawing of Dr Carroll did have something to do with Anna. She was mature and attractive and efficient, just the sort of woman you'd expect him to be interested in. Her own foolish fancy quickly evaporated, without rancour, and she returned to her task with a resigned shrug. If she was going to daydream about doctors, she'd better stick to intern Tom Rolfe. At least he had asked her out. . .

Dr Carroll *had* taken a fancy to Sister Mackay, and it was worrying him. He felt a little ashamed of his brash behaviour on Friday night and suspected that her stiffness with him today was because of it. She was probably feeling a little bit ashamed herself for allowing him to take even such minor liberties as he had. Anna, he believed, was not prim, but perhaps not as fully aware of her sexuality as she'd imagined. Or he'd imagined. She'd given him a bit of a jolt, and it had been her instinctive response that had made him assume too much.

All the time they were with the patients he was strongly aware of her trim but voluptuous figure close beside him, the faint flowery perfume that clung to her, not from scent but from some soap or shampoo she used. She had had the same aura on Friday when he had disturbed her just out of her bath. Glancing at her, his eyes stripped away the neat pale blue uniform and replaced it with the blue velour dressing-gown that had so invitingly fallen open, and he ached suddenly to feel those small but strong hands on his body again. . . It had been a long time since he'd made love to a woman, so long that probably no one would believe in his abstinence. But after Janis, Scott had retreated physically and mentally from women, instinctively shying away from any kind of involvement, until one morning he'd knocked a girl off her bicycle and now, for some unknown reason, he seemed to have a dilemma. He'd better be careful, he advised himself. She wasn't the kind of woman he wanted to get involved with.

Back in her office some time later, Scott checked over prescriptions and instructions for the care of his various patients. Anna ordered tea and they conferred at length. Anna had at first been a little miffed by his attention to detail—and had been more than once tempted to tell him that nurses did know a thing or two about caring for patients, that they did several years' training in the art and did not have to have all the 'i's dotted and 't's crossed, but she had balked at aggravating him unnecessarily. Now she was more inclined to admire him for his thoroughness.

Finally he said, 'Well, I think that's all.' He drained his cup and asked, 'Any more tea in that pot?'

Anna reached for it. 'I think so.' She refilled his cup and there was enough for her too.

'Did you go bushwalking at the weekend?' Scott enquired.

'No.'

His eyes narrowed a little. 'Other things to do?'

Anna tossed her head and said lightly, 'There's always plenty to do.'

'You've got a string of boyfriends, I suppose?' He wondered why he'd asked that. It was of no interest to him whether she had one or a hundred.

'Dozens!' She gave him a dry look. 'None, actually.

When my mother was alive I didn't have time for much social activity—whatever I had, I had with her.'

Scott realised that all weekend he'd been imagining her with some other man, and now, alarmingly, he was relieved to find she hadn't been. 'Except bushwalking.'

Anna nodded. 'She insisted I take up some interest that didn't involve her. We needed to have time away from each other. She played bridge.'

'There's a walk next weekend,' Scott dropped the unplanned remark in casually. 'Are you going?'

'I might,' she answered cautiously.

'I might too,' he said, fixing her with penetrating grey eyes. 'Especially if you say you'll have dinner with me afterwards.' He wasn't sure if he was in his right mind, but she was proving irresistible.

'I don't know if. . .'

'I won't be as ungallant as I was on Friday,' Scott promised.

Anna smiled. 'Were you ungallant?'

'I perhaps deserved to have my face slapped, but you're too ladylike to do such a thing.'

'Perhaps I should have.'

There was a pause. 'You haven't answered the question,' he reminded her.

'Well, I did rather enjoy the Winston pub,' Anna said carefully.

'Another time, maybe,' said Scott. 'I was thinking of changing and driving to Ballarat for a meal. There's a bigger choice of restaurants than in Mount William.' It could be regarded as a kind of apology, he rationalised.

'And less likelihood of being seen,' she remarked.

'Anna, it isn't that I don't want to be seen with you,' he told her at once. 'It's just that—well, I like my privacy when I'm off duty. I'm not the fraternising type.'

'Neither am I,' Anna said. 'I didn't mean it the way you took it.'

Scott glanced at his watch. 'I'd better go—I've got a couple of male patients to look at. We had a prostatectomy that proved to be a tricky one this morning.'

Anna said, 'I hope your back will be better by Sunday.'

'So do I, but walking will probably be good for it.'

For Anna it was suddenly a long week. Things quietened down at the hospital, and although she should have been delighted not to be rushed off her feet she found herself having more time to think about Sunday. That she was looking forward to it there was no doubt, but was going out with Scott Carroll wise? Several times she asked herself this question, and never really got a satisfactory answer.

Scott appeared on the ward as usual, was demanding and sometimes critical, but to Anna he seemed different. Less abrasive, she thought, as though he was thinking first before slamming into someone, pulling himself up. He still had them all on their toes, but there was a subtle difference, she felt, and wondered if others noticed too.

By Friday Meg certainly had.

'How'd you tame Carroll?' she demanded, when they were sharing a midnight mug of cocoa as they occasionally did if Anna had not gone to bed early.

Anna laughed. 'Is he tame?'

'Well, it suddenly occurred to me today that I'd been getting on with him better,' Meg admitted. 'He does seem to have mellowed.'

'Maybe you did the taming.'

'You must have noticed,' Meg said, eyeing her house-mate narrowly.

Anna felt guilty because she hadn't confided in Meg, but somehow she couldn't. Not just because she didn't want to break a confidence, but because she didn't want Meg asking probing questions about her own feelings towards the registrar.

'Perhaps he is a little less abrasive lately,' Anna said carefully. 'Maybe he just took time to settle in, Meg, to get used to us and for us to get used to him.'

'Yes, I suppose so,' Meg conceded. 'I suppose we do tend to take people at face value rather too readily and judge them arbitrarily. Maybe whatever it was that was bugging him has been resolved.' She grinned. 'Are you sure it isn't your doing?'

'Have a heart!' protested Anna.

'Well, you do go bushwalking together.'

'Once!' Anna bit her lip and felt bound to confess, 'Well, he's going this weekend, I gather, but. . .'

'And you're not staying home. Well, why should you? If you fancy the man, go for it, Anna. He's good-looking, clever, and can probably whisk you away from all this eventually if he's a mind to.' Meg gave a dramatic sigh.

'You're fantasising!'

'Which you, of course, never do! Come on, Anna, don't be coy. I won't tell. *Do* you fancy him?'

'I have a great deal of admiration for him,' Anna confessed, still wondering whether to say anything about having dinner with Scott. Somehow she still didn't want to admit to too close a relationship, because Meg would be bound to read volumes into it.

Meg threw her knitting down and drained her cocoa. 'I think you're falling in love with him.'

'That's a typical remark from a lovesick woman,' Anna said, laughing.

'Well, I should know,' said Meg seriously.

'How's your remance with Peter?' Anna asked. 'When do you see him? You're on duty most evenings. Why don't you try and change to a day shift for a while?'

Meg picked up her knitting again. 'Oh, it's all part of the excitement—snatching time together when he comes up to the hospital, meeting him for lunch, and of course there are my weekends off.' She trailed away blissfully. 'Weekends are wonderful!'

'I did kind of gather that.' Anna gathered up the mugs and yawned. 'I'm for bed.' She paused in the doorway. 'Are you two going to get married?'

Meg looked at her with a wistful expression. 'I hope so. Ask me again in a week or two.'

On Saturday night Meg did not come home after a date with Peter. She had warned Anna. 'Don't send out search parties,' she'd said offhandedly. 'It might turn out to be embarrassing!'

Anna was still awake long after midnight, not worrying about Meg, but thinking about her own date with Scott the following day. He had naturally insisted on picking her up, but that was not what was teasing her mind. It was the thought of having dinner with him as a more formal arrangement than the previous occasion, and wondering how she would cope with the consequences.

Scott arrived early on Sunday morning, and Anna was glad that Meg was still asleep. She was on duty

that evening and probably would have left by the time
Scott drove Anna home to change and then picked her
up again later. It wasn't that she didn't want Meg to
know about her activities, but that she was afraid Meg
might say something offputting, particularly in view of
the romantic state she was in.

Anna was ready to go when Scott arrived. She was
wearing her green parka and brown trousers, sturdy
bushwalking boots, and carrying a backpack containing
lunch for both of them which she had insisted on
preparing in return for the lift he was giving her.

Her hair was neatly coiled and pushed under a
peaked cap and she had bought herself some binoculars. Scott looked her over approvingly as she slid into
the passenger seat, then remarked on the binoculars
hanging around her neck.

'You took my advice and got eight by forty.'

'Yes. I think they're quite good ones.'

He lifted them for closer inspection, which brought
him closer to her, almost, she thought, close enough to
kiss. . . 'Fairly expensive, by the look of them.' He
smiled. 'Let's hope we see some birds to justify the
expense!'

It was almost a disappointing day. Anna enjoyed the
walking, she enjoyed Scott's company and the way he
was content to go for miles without saying much, unless
to draw her attention to some bird or other. It was
companionable, and for most of the time she almost
forgot about the other members of the party. But there
was no waterfall where they stopped for lunch, no
creek to be helped across, and no magic moment all
alone with Scott like the time before. They were more
a part of the group this time, and Anna felt that in
some way she had been cheated.

You fool, she told herself, as she snatched a quick shower before changing to go out again. What's the matter with you?

For dining out, she chose a pink wool dress and loose-fitting jacket. She let her hair hang loose and added a little eyeshadow to her make-up. She was just sliding her feet into black patent court shoes when the doorbell rang. She picked up her black patent handbag and hurried to answer it.

Scott looked suave in a navy suit and pale blue shirt. He was freshly shaved, Anna noticed, and his hair was slicked back and still damp. He smelled of an astringently masculine aftershave. He showed no sign of back trouble until getting into the car, when his face twitched slightly as he slid behind the wheel.

'Your back still troubling you?' Anna asked in surprise.

'The occasional twinge,' he admitted, 'when I move awkwardly. Incipient arthritis, I suppose.' He turned to smile at her. 'I'm not as young as I used to be.'

'Oh, hark at the old man!' she joked, and the slight constraint which had seemed between them faded as Scott grinned at her.

He seemed to know his way around Ballarat as he did around everywhere else, and Anna found herself ushered into a restaurant she hadn't even known existed, although she was fairly familiar with many of the local venues. It was a small intimate place and their table was in a far corner against a wall.

For a while they talked about bushwalking and some of the people in the group, then inevitably the conversation turned to the hospital and the patients, despite Scott's previous reluctance to talk shop.

After one fairly lively discussion about the treatment

Scott proposed for a patient with kidney stones, he suddenly leaned back and laughed. 'Anna, you really must take up medicine again. It's obvious you're hankering to be a doctor. You're wasted nursing.'

Anna wasn't so positive. 'Not wasted. . .'

'You know what I mean. You're not fulfilling your potential.' He leaned forward again. 'If you want to get into a medical school for next year, you'd better get a move on. You need to get your application in now, otherwise you'll have to wait another year.'

Anna realised it was foolish to procrastinate, but she was still indecisive. 'Scott, I don't know. . .'

He frowned. 'Anna, stop procrastinating! Now is the time to choose which road to take. Do you want to be a doctor or not?'

Anna moistened her lips and met his determined gaze. 'Yes,' she said, 'I do.'

He smiled. 'Good. Now as you've already done one year and your nursing training, it's on the cards you might be able to get accepted in second year and avoid repeating first year.'

Anna was greatly heartened by this possibility. 'Really?'

'If you've got the right subjects, and your marks were good.'

Suddenly the prospect seemed less daunting. She told him everything he wanted to know about her training and her exam results, and was encouraged by his certainty that she stood a good chance of being accepted into second-year medicine.

'It's not just your qualifications, though,' he said, frowning. 'There aren't usually many places for second-year entrants.' He stroked his cheek thoughtfully, then said, 'Look, if you like I'll arrange an interview with someone who'll tell you what your chances are. Could you go to Melbourne for a couple of days?'

'Only at weekends—I'm off most weekends. I do a weekend shift only about once a month or in an emergency.' She smiled. 'I work more or less civilised hours.'

'Then I'll arrange it and we'll go.'

'We. . .?' she queried.

'It's about time I whizzed down to see how the place is surviving without me.'

Anna was excited, but felt things were moving too fast. 'That's very kind, Scott, and I do appreciate your egging me on like this, but I'm not sure I'm cut out to be a doctor.'

He caught hold of her hand and said earnestly, 'You sound a lot like young Liz Farmer! I think maybe your self-esteem needs a bit of a boost too. Don't be too self-effacing, Anna. You've got what it takes, believe me, and it's a shame to see a talent wasted—all right, not wasted, just not developed.'

'You're very flattering.'

'Do you agree to go?' he asked bluntly.

Anna bit her lip. 'All right—yes. I'll meet this person you suggest.'

'Professor John Carter. He's Professor of Surgery at Melbourne Uni. A very astute man, brilliant surgeon. You'll like him.'

'I'm terrified already!'

Scott clasped her hand tightly. 'Don't worry, you have a way of taming tigers.'

Anna blushed. 'Thank you for doing this for me, Scott. I'm really grateful.'

It was late when they arrived home and Anna was hesitant about asking Scott in for coffee in case he should interpret it wrongly. But not to seemed ungrateful. In the end, she said, 'I know it's late, but if you'd like a coffee. . .'

'You have to be up early,' he said, 'so I won't keep you. I'm going to be busy myself tomorrow.' He'd been rather quiet on the way home, and Anna had sensed a withdrawal as she had before. She hoped he wasn't regretting his offer to help her.

'Thank you for dinner,' she said. 'I enjoyed it very much.'

He turned to her, almost reluctantly, it seemed. 'So did I.' Their eyes held for too long. The spark ignited and Scott reached for her with a swift decisive movement, pulling her away from the passenger door and tightly into his arms. 'Coffee at this time of night is bad for you,' he chided huskily, 'but this isn't. . .' And he kissed her, gently at first, then with mounting passion, invading her mouth with a sensuousness that took her breath away.

'Anna. . .' he breathed against her neck as his hand fumbled with the buttons on the bodice of her dress, then cupped her breast warmly in his palm. 'Anna, you're so lovely. . . I'm trying not to, but I can't help wanting you. . .'

And I'm a fool, she thought muzzily, letting him do this, but I can't help it. I'm in love with him and I don't care. . . The realisation came suddenly and shocked her for a moment. She slid her arms around him, pulling out his shirt so that she could make contact with the bare skin of his back, and offering her lips to him with an ardour she had never known she possessed.

'Maybe I should come in for coffee after all,' Scott murmured against her ear.

Anna's mind and body insisted yes, yes, come in

with me. . .but her common sense roused itself. An affair with Scott Carroll was not what she wanted. And there was nothing else he would offer. He was a man avoiding commitment, a man disappointed in love once and not likely to try it again. Not yet, anyway. She'd have to take him on his terms, and she wasn't sure she was strong enough to do that. The bliss of a temporary liaison—for that was all it would be—would not be worth the heartbreak that would follow.

Before Anna could answer, headlights came down the road and a car turned into the driveway. Meg had come home, even later than usual. She tooted rudely, and at once the spell was broken. Hurriedly Anna buttoned her dress and opened the passenger door, astonished that she had even contemplated for a second sneaking him into the house right under Meg's very nose. 'Goodnight, Scott,' she said. 'And thanks again. . .'

He grasped her hand and held it to his lips. 'Don't forget to let me know which weekend you can go to Melbourne.'

Anna didn't answer. She pulled her hand away, slid out of the car, slamming the door behind her, and ran after Meg into the house.

CHAPTER EIGHT

'HEY, look at you!' Meg exclaimed in surprise, when Anna came into the hall. 'All dressed up! Where have you been? Sorry if I interrupted anything, but you didn't have to mind me. . .' She chuckled and peered more closely at Anna's face. 'I wonder who's been kissing you!'

Anna could not get out of explanations now. 'Scott suggested we change after the bushwalk and go to Ballarat for dinner.'

'Wow!' Meg was impressed.

'Meg, don't talk about it, will you?' Anna begged. 'At the hospital, I mean. I don't want anyone to think. . .'

Meg shook her head. 'Not a word shall pass my lips.' She smiled widely. 'Well, I never! Anna Mackay and Dr Carroll—whoever would have thought it?'

'Look, there's nothing to it,' Anna said earnestly. 'A date, a goodnight kiss.' She shrugged. 'I probably won't go out with him again.' Already she was wishing she hadn't said she'd go to Melbourne with Scott. Her feelings towards him would make her much too vulnerable.

'Bit fresh, was he?' Meg said bluntly, noting that Anna's buttons were done up unevenly.

'You know what men are,' Anna said lightly. She walked down the hall. 'Want a hot drink?'

Meg followed her to the kitchen and switched on the electric heater. She was very curious about Anna's date, but Anna was soon able to divert her into talking about the wonderful Peter.

'He asked me to marry him last night,' Meg said softly.

Anna was scarcely surprised. 'And you said yes?'

Meg looked up, starry-eyed. 'Is there any other word?' She jumped up and whirled around the kitchen. 'Anna, I'm so happy I could burst!'

'Not in the kitchen, please!' joked Anna. She added sincerely, 'That's wonderful, Meg. I'm really happy for you. Peter's a great person.'

Meg subsided into a chair and clasped the mug of cocoa Anna handed to her. 'It's such a fantastic feeling. And Peter's so considerate and gentle. . . Hell, Anna, I had no idea what it was all about before I met him. OK, I've not been all that pure. I've hopped into bed with guys I liked on occasions, but it was never like this. Love makes all the difference. Peter says so too. . .' She paused, grimacing. 'I hope I don't make him sound soppy, because he isn't. He's. . .'

'Really quite macho,' teased Anna, feeling a twinge of envy. She was happy for her friend, but Meg's radiance made her feel more than a little wistful. After all he'd said, she'd be a fool to think that Scott Carroll would ever want more than an affair with her.

Meg sobered. 'Anna, I've been worrying about you all day.'

'Me? Why?'

'Well, Peter and I aim to get married quite soon, and we'll be living in his flat, at least until we build or buy a place of our own. He likes Mount William and so do I, so we aim to stay for a while anyway, and it'll be more sensible to own our own place rather than rent.'

'What you're saying is that shortly you'll want to

move out of here?' Anna realised that she should have been expecting it.

Meg looked at her with mute appeal. Finally she said, 'We're going to be married in a few weeks, Anna. I'm sorry it's not giving you much notice, but—well, everything just *happened*.'

Anna took the empty mugs and rinsed them. She felt suddenly that everything was overtaking her. Perhaps this was the catalyst, she thought, this and falling in love with Scott Carroll. She'd felt she was at a crossroads, and even tonight she had still been dithering about which road to take, but now the way seemed to be signposted. Perhaps she *was* meant to go back to medicine.

She turned, leaning on the sink. 'I've just about made up my mind to take up medicine again,' she said. 'Scott's offered to introduce me to a professor down in Melbourne, to talk it over. Things are a little different from England here. I don't know yet whether I'll have to start right at the beginning again or if I can make a lateral entry into second year. If I do get accepted in a medical school, I'll have to move at the end of the year anyway. You needn't worry about the rent in the meantime. I can afford to keep the house on until I go.'

Meg looked relieved. 'I was hoping you might have reached a decision. I'm glad, Anna. You're a terrific nurse, but I think you've got what it takes to be an even better doctor.' She grinned. 'I don't envy you, mind. You've got a long haul ahead.'

'I know. That's why I've been so undecided. It's a massive commitment, especially at my age.'

'Obviously Scott's been encouraging you,' Meg observed.

'He says I've got to hurry up and apply if I want to start next year. That's why he offered to introduce me to this professor of surgery friend of his.'

Meg tilted her head enquiringly. 'Sounds as if he wants to make sure you're down in Melbourne next year!'

Anna was startled by this assumption. It hadn't occurred to her and she didn't think it likely. She shook her head. 'I don't think so. He's just being helpful.'

'Are you in love with him?' Meg asked bluntly.

Anna tried hard not to give herself away. 'No, of course not,' she said, forcing a laugh. 'Anyway, he'll still be here until the middle of next year.'

'It might be a different story once you meet up again, though,' Meg said. 'Absence makes the heart grow fonder, you know.'

Anna was adamant. 'I shan't have time for romance—I'll need every minute for study, and I won't be able to afford distractions.' Being in love with Scott was an aberration, she decided, one she would soon get over if she behaved sensibly. She was calling mere physical attraction love, that was the trouble. Once she was out of his orbit, she would soon forget him.

Meg smiled. 'That's a pity, because you and he would go well together, I reckon.'

It was three weeks before Scott drove Anna to Melbourne to meet John Carter. For Anna it had been a time of personal anxiety as she vacillated between wanting to take the plunge, if it were possible, and being afraid of it. Scott seemed to sense her dilemma and went out of his way to be encouraging. He insisted she obtain application forms and helped her to fill them in.

'We'll do one in rough as a trial run,' he said. 'So you can show it to John Carter.'

Although Anna appreciated his interest and help, the more he tried to persuade her that going back to medicine was the right course for her, the more she had to accept that his feelings towards her were merely physical. Scott Carroll did not intend to become involved with a woman, and especially not a career woman. His wife Janis had made sure of that.

They went bushwalking twice during the ensuing weekends, and on both occasions ended up having tea at the Winston pub. It went without saying that Scott gave Anna a lift to these outings. In any case, both were further afield than it would have been convenient to ride her bicycle, and she would have had to beg a lift with someone. She could have found an excuse not to go, but she was not that strong. She couldn't say no to Scott, she enjoyed being with him too much.

She must just be careful, she told herself, not to get any fanciful ideas about him. She must not let herself be influenced by Meg, whose starry-eyed radiance was all-pervading these days. Scott Carroll was not Peter Robbins.

Anna prepared for the trip to Melbourne with feelings that were a mixture of misgivings and excitement. Now that she had taken this positive step in the direction of taking up medicine again, the old feeling of elation gripped her as it had when she had first walked into a lecture theatre at the start of her first year at medical school. Suddenly the years ahead had ceased to seem formidable, and now it was the same. She knew she would become so totally absorbed that the time would pass quickly. Even if they did not save her a year's study, her nursing training and experience would stand her in good stead, she knew, help to make a great many aspects more immediately clear, and easier to learn. And having been a nurse, she would surely be a more understanding and considerate doctor.

Scott evidently thought so. 'You'll have a great advantage knowing the nursing side of things,' he said, as they were driving down the Western Highway towards the city. He turned briefly to smile at her. 'You'll be able to appreciate nurses more than we male chauvinist medicos!'

'I hope so!' she rejoined with fervour. 'At least I'll know what goes on, how hard nurses work. I hope I won't be as condescending as some doctors are.'

'Ouch! Did I deserve that?'

'No. You're not condescending, just a bit brusque at times,' Anna told him. She added boldly, with humour in her tone, 'But you've improved.'

He pulled a face. 'Thanks, I'm sure!' Another side-long glance and a smile showed he was not annoyed by what she'd said. 'Do they still call me The Ogre behind my back?'

She laughed. 'I'm not aware that the title was generally used. Meg said she thought you must have got over whatever was bugging you, but everyone else seems to have taken any change in their stride. I didn't tell Meg anything about—about your wife, of course.' She added, 'Of course your demanding such high standards has just resulted in everyone trying hard not to give you any cause for complaint. And I suppose there's nothing wrong with that.'

'I try not to bite people's heads off,' he said contritely.

'You don't—often,' Anna said honestly.

Scott laughed softly. 'Sister Mackay, I don't think

you know how good you are for me. Your honesty is very refreshing, and yet you manage to sound so diplomatic even when you're telling me a home truth.' He released one hand from the wheel and placed it briefly on her thigh. A sharp bend in the road required him to restore it to the wheel, for which Anna was grateful. Whenever Scott touched her, accidentally or not, she experienced much too strong a reaction.

'I apologise if I've been rude,' she said.

'Rude! You've been a tonic, Anna. Just what I needed.' He glanced at her again. 'The trouble is you're too damned attractive. I keep wanting to make love to you. You don't know how hard it is to keep my distance, to let things go so far and no further.'

'I'm sorry. . .it's not fair to frustrate you,' said Anna. 'We shouldn't go out together. But I. . .'

'You don't go to bed with any old Tom, Dick or Harry, I know,' Scott said, with a touch of impatience. 'I respect that, Anna. You're the kind of woman to give herself to the man she falls in love with, and no one else.'

'A bit old-fashioned of me,' she murmured.

'That's one of the things which makes you so attractive,' said Scott, with a quirk of amusement flicking across his mouth. 'You know, Anna, I could easily fall in love with you. . .' At her sharp intake of breath, he went on, 'But don't worry, I won't. I've no intention of getting involved with anyone right now. Once was enough. And if I ever do, you can bet she'll be right outside the medical profession and preferably a home-body. No more clashing careers, thank you.'

'That's probably wise,' commented Anna, with a leaden feeling in her stomach. If Scott loved me, I wouldn't think twice about a career, she thought with absolute conviction. I wouldn't care if I never became a doctor. She wondered what he would say if she voiced the thought, but didn't dare to. He was only talking idly.

They stopped for lunch in Ballarat and were in Melbourne late afternoon. Scott had booked rooms at a motel near Melbourne University. Anna was sure he could have stayed with friends if he'd wanted to, but had chosen the motel so that she would not feel abandoned.

Her appointment with Professor Carter was on Sunday morning at the professor's house on elegant tree-lined Royal Parade.

'You must have people you want to see,' Anna said to Scott, after they'd checked in. 'Don't worry about me tonight. I'll be all right. It's not the first time I've been to Melbourne. I'll probably go to the cinema.'

He clamped a hand on her shoulder. 'If you desperately want to be alone and independent, by all means, but if you can stand my company why don't we go together?'

She looked up at him. The grey eyes were smiling, teasing her a little. Her heart quickened. 'Well, of course I'd like that.'

She changed into the smart blue suit she had brought to wear tomorrow morning for her visit to Professor Carter, and was glad she had when Scott appeared in a suit. He looked very handsome, very debonair, she thought, and ached to reach up and kiss him.

As though he had read her mind he cupped her face in his large hands and tilted her mouth to his, brushing her lips lightly. His eyes smouldered for a moment, as his fingers slid under her hair and caressed her nape.

'Anna, why do you tantalise me so? It isn't fair! I

want you like crazy, and you're as unattainable as the moon.'

Not if you loved me, she whispered in her heart.

'Come on,' he said, 'before I forget all my good resolutions.'

It was a small, secluded restaurant that he took her to, on the city's fringe. It was expensive, Anna noticed, glancing down the menu, very up-market. She was glad she'd worn her good suit. A gypsy violinist played and sang plaintive songs in the background and the service was swift and attentive. Anna felt undeservedly pampered.

Scott was more talkative than usual. Anna found that they had common views about a great many things besides medicine and bushwalking. In fact they scarcely mentioned the hospital or medical topics, and a casual remark of hers concerning bushwalking led them into deep discussion of environmental issues. They were both, Anna discovered with some gratification, members of Greenpeace.

Finally Scott looked at his watch and said, 'We talk too much. Now we're too late for the cinema.'

'Never mind. There wasn't anything I particularly wanted to see. I've enjoyed talking just as much.'

He smiled and placed his hand over hers. 'Thanks for the compliment. You're very easy to talk to, Anna.'

'All part of the therapy,' she said, then wished she hadn't, because it sounded flip, and she hadn't meant it that way.

He said rather wistfully, 'Janis and I never talked much. After the first few months we never seemed to be together long enough to have a real conversation.'

'I've heard about married couples who converse via notes stuck on the fridge,' Anna mused.

For a moment his expression was withdrawn, then he seemed to snap back as though by an effort of will. 'Shall we have another coffee? he asked. 'And then I think you'd better have an early night. You'll want your wits about you in the morning if you're to make a good impression on old John.'

'I'm nervous,' Anna confessed. She added, 'Yes, I would like more coffee. Thanks.'

As the waitress withdrew from their table after taking the order, a woman approached. She was slightly behind Scott, so he didn't notice her at once. Anna watched the tall, slender woman in black with short-cropped blonde hair with a sudden sinking feeling. She did not know her, but presumably Scott did. The woman was very attractive in a sharp-featured way, and had an air of complete self-assurance. She stared for a moment at Anna as she paused just behind Scott's chair, then she dropped her hand on his shoulder.

'Scott!'

As her meticulously manicured fingers drummed ever so slightly on the smooth cloth covering Scott's shoulder, it struck Anna as odd that her nails were not painted, since her face was perfectly made up.

Scott was clearly startled, but he showed little outward sign of it. He turned slightly, glancing up at the newcomer. Not a shred of emotion showed in his face. 'Hello, Janis.'

Janis! Scott's wife. A strange feeling crept over Anna and she recognised it with dismay—jealousy.

'I thought you were holed up in the wilds of the Wimmera,' Janis Carroll drawled silkily, surveying him critically as though it was bound to have affected his health.

'Not the Wimmera,' he replied evenly. 'Mount William, the Central Highlands.'

Janis waved a hand dismissively. 'I was never much good at geography. Country Victoria somewhere, I heard.' She treated Anna to a similarly critical gaze, and Scott said,

'Anna, this is my wife, Janis. Janis, Sister Mackay from Mount William Hospital.'

Janis smiled thinly, and Anna muttered, 'How do you do?' She felt she ought to vapourise, that that was what Janis would like. The woman looked from her to Scott and back, her suspicions very clearly stated in her eyes.

'Mind if I join you?' Janis asked, reaching behind her to take a chair from an empty table. 'I haven't had dessert or coffee yet.'

Scott had risen to move the chair. He said, 'Aren't you with someone?' His eyes flicked across the restaurant.

'A couple of girl friends,' Janis said lightly. 'They can spare me for a while.'

He sent a quick apologetic glance in Anna's direction, which she interpreted as meaning he would appreciate it if she left them. She was delighted to. Janis Carroll and Anna Mackay clearly had nothing to say to each other.

So she said, 'If you don't mind, Scott, I'll be going. I'm rather tired. It's all right, I'll get them to call a taxi for me.'

He seemed to be resolving some conflict within for a moment or two, but finally he said, 'All right.' He called the waitress over and asked her to bring the menu for Janis, and to order a taxi for Anna. There were a painful few minutes before the taxi arrived and

Anna was able to escape. Janis Carroll used the time to learn as much about Anna as she could, and was openly sceptical about her chances of getting a place next year in first year, let alone second. Janis was clearly not impressed by nurses who wanted to become doctors.

Anna went to bed as soon as she returned to the motel, but sleep was impossible. She eventually turned on the light and tried to read the novel she had shoved in her overnight bag. Concentrating on the words was equally impossible, and she lay staring at the ceiling, plagued by images of Scott and Janis, convinced they would have left the restaurant together. She must have slipped into a light doze eventually, because she surfaced to a light rap on her door.

'Are you awake, Anna?' It was Scott.

'Yes, what is it?'

'I want to talk to you for a minute.'

Anna slid out of bed, shrugged into her dressing-gown, and padded to the door. Scott looked so forlorn that she wanted to take him in her arms and comfort him. 'Come in,' she invited.

'I saw your light on and wondered if you were still awake,' he said. 'I felt I had to apologise.'

'You might as well sit down.' Anna indicated the armchair. She perched on the edge of the bed, drawing her dressing-gown more tightly around her. 'There's no need to apologise. It was obviously an awkward situation, and I could see you wanted me to go.'

He raked a hand through his hair. 'I didn't! I wanted you to stay so she wouldn't!'

'You surely don't need moral support to talk to your wife!' She sounded arch, but couldn't help it.

'Listen,' he said, leaning forward, his head in his

hands. 'It was a shock to see her there. I haven't seen her for months. We've only communicated through solicitors. I thought she was probably in America by now, but apparently it all fell through.' He looked at Anna in anguish. 'Just as the divorce is about to come through, she's talking about a reconciliation.'

'Why?' Anna's heart felt like stone.

'That's it—I don't know. She's so evasive, so plausible.'

'It's a bit sudden, isn't it? Why hasn't she been in touch with you?'

'She says she was afraid to, but seeing me there tonight gave her courage. . .'

'And what are you going to do?' Anna asked quietly.

'I don't know. . .'

'You're still in love with her, aren't you?'

He shook his head. 'No. . .hell, I don't know. . .it's a mess, Anna. I don't know how I feel about anything. I know I don't want to go through that nightmare again, but. . .'

'Maybe she's changed. Maybe things will be different now. Maybe you can talk things over, make compromises on both sides.'

He gave a wan smile. 'Maybe you should be a marriage guidance counsellor!'

'Maybe you should sleep on it, Scott. Don't rush into anything. See her a few times, get to know her again.'

'But I'm stuck up at Mount William for a year.'

'It's not so far to drive to Melbourne. Maybe she could come up there sometimes.'

'No, it wouldn't work,' he said raggedly. 'I'm a fool even to think about it.'

'There's no harm in thinking. Just don't act rashly.'

'I've always been too impulsive,' he admitted. 'That was how I married Janis in the first place.'

'Well, perhaps now's the time to take stock and start all over again. Are you seeing her again this weekend?'

'She wants to have lunch with me tomorrow,' he confessed. 'I told her I might not be able to.'

'Of course you'll be able to. You don't have to consider me, Scott. I can look after myself. I'll wander around the art gallery and the botanic gardens. Just tell me what time you want to leave and where to meet you.'

He studied her for a moment or two. 'You're so matter-of-fact, so calm, but it's easy for you, you're not involved. . .'

Anna kept her expression blank while her emotions churned painfully. Not involved! She was in love with the man. And he was going to jump out of the frying-pan right back into the fire, she feared. There was nothing she could do about it. Scott had to work out his destiny for himself. She guessed he was tempted to go back to Janis because that would assuage his deep sense of failure, at least temporarily. But how long would it last? One glimpse of Janis told Anna not long. Janis would use him as she'd used him before. Her overseas job had fallen through, she was out on a limb, and suddenly Scott had fallen back into her lap. It was hardly surprising, especially as he'd been with another woman, that she had thought about reconciliation. Anna had no doubts about how she would present it to her friends, that Scott had begged her to go back to him. Couldn't he see that?

'Would you like a nightcap?' she asked. 'There are all sorts of miniatures in the fridge.'

A faint smile temporarily relaxed Scott's features.

'Yeah—I guess I need one.' He crossed to her refrigerator and opened it. 'What do you fancy?'

'I don't know that I should. . .'

'Don't let me drink alone! Just one—how about a brandy?'

'All right.'

There were glasses on top of the fridge and he poured the contents of a brandy miniature into one, whisky into the other, and splashed a little ginger ale in each.

Anna spluttered as she tried it. 'More ginger ale, please!'

Scott sat on the end of the bed and faced her. 'No more of my problems. What a nerve I've got, tipping them on you! I'm sorry, Anna, I shouldn't have disturbed you, but I was so angry that you'd felt you had to go. I felt despicable. . .'

Instinctively she leaned towards him and covered his hand which lay palm down on the bed. 'I wish you'd stop apologising.'

'All right. I said no more about me. Let's talk about you. Tomorrow. I'll drive you to John's place in the morning—about ten-fifteen, he said, and I'll pick you up where?'

'What time do you want to go back?'

'We ought to leave about five at the latest, I suppose.'

'Well, what about the arts centre? I could meet you there. I can wait inside.'

He stood up and paced the room. 'No, this is monstrous. I'll tell Janis I can't make it,' he said firmly. 'I'm not going to leave you to your own devices all day.'

'Yes, you are,' she insisted. 'You're going to see

Janis and talk things over. It's an opportunity you
might not have again, Scott. Better to do it now before
the divorce is final. I'm a big girl, quite used to
meandering round a city on my own. Your meeting
Janis is more important than entertaining me. You've
done quite enough for me, anyway, arranging for me
to see Professor Carter.'

He looked doubtful, but she could see he wanted to
accept what she'd said. Finally he capitulated. 'All
right. And thanks, Anna. Thanks a million.'

'You can tell me all about it on the way home,' she
said, with a touch of irony she hoped he wouldn't
notice.

He downed the whisky and put his empty glass on
the bench. Anna placed her drink on the bedside table,
hardly touched. Scott said, 'I guess I'd better turn in.'

'See you in the morning.' Anna rose to open the
door, and found him already halfway there, blocking
her way. She paused.

For a moment they stood looking at each other,
uncertain, emotion flowing between them, then Scott
drew her into his arms. 'Anna, I wish it was you. . .'
He broke off, and held her hard against him. His
breath stirred her hair and his heart beat strongly
against her. Anna wanted him to kiss her, but knew he
would not, not tonight, perhaps never again. Perhaps
it was better this way. If Scott went back to his wife,
then she might be able to forget him more easily.

Feeling tears suddenly starting, and not trusting her
self-control to hold, she drew back. 'Goodnight, Scott.
And don't worry about it. It'll work out, I'm sure.' She
sounded trite, but what else was there to say?

He dragged his fingers up through her hair, touching

her scalp and sending shivers of fire right through her, then softly kissed her mouth, a mere gesture of gratitude.

'Goodnight, Anna. And thanks.'

CHAPTER NINE

'THIS is one of those decisions I would rather not have had to make,' Scott said gravely, replacing the X-rays on Anna's desk.

Anna's chest constricted. 'Amputation?'

'I'm afraid so.'

She drew in a deep breath. 'Have you told her?'

He nodded. 'She took it very well, even made a joke about being "Long Joan Silver", but of course she's shattered, they always are. I suggested going to Melbourne for a second opinion, but she seems willing to accept my prognosis. I told her I'd consulted a cardio-vascular surgeon who, on the basis of her history and these X-rays, agreed with me, and was willing to take her as a patient, but she doesn't want to go away from home.'

'They never do at her age,' observed Anna. 'But she might need to for prosthesis.'

Scott looked thoughtful. 'That shouldn't be necessary. Isn't there a travelling service?'

She wasn't sure. 'I really don't know—I've never had occasion to since I've been here. Matron will know, of course.'

'Well, if there isn't,' Scott said decisively, 'we'll have to arrange something.'

Anna smiled. It was typical of him to show such consideration for patients, especially elderly ones like Joan Silver, who was in her seventies. She'd lived all her life in Mount William and was determined that if

she was going to die it was going to be there. She was
the widow of a local farmer, and when he'd died a year
previously she had moved into a retirement unit in the
town.

'And there I'll stay till they carry me out in a box,'
she'd said to Anna the day she had been admitted with
severe claudication in her left leg which had some
months before received arterial grafting. She was a
friendly, cheerful person who always seemed more
concerned about the medical problems of her fellow
patients than her own. Anna had developed quite an
affection for her in a very short time.

Scott dragged a weary hand across his brow. He had
looked very strained since their weekend in
Melbourne, and Anna guessed that the emotional
pressure on him in his personal life was still intense.
She longed to help, to comfort, to do anything to take
the stress from his face, but he had become very
withdrawn since that weekend. He had not once confided in her since, perhaps not wanting to burden her
with his problems, but more likely, she assumed,
because his dilemma had become just too intensely
personal. He had said very little in the car on the
return journey from Melbourne, and she had not
probed. That day he had kept the conversation mainly
to her interview with Professor Carter.

Scott had driven her to the Royal Parade address,
lingering only to introduce her to the professor and
make apologies about having to dash off on urgent
business. The tall, distinguished surgeon with the shock
of white hair had instantly captivated Anna with a
welcoming smile that dissipated all her nerves. The
next hour had flown, and at the end of it she had lost
any misgivings she might have had about going back to

medicine. John Carter was an inspiration. And his wife, a doctor herself, who joined them for morning tea, made Anna feel she would be selling herself short if she did not become a doctor. They both offered to help smooth her path to medical school in any way they could, and urged her to lodge her application straight away.

Scott was referred to only once, when Madeleine Carter remarked, 'Such a shame, Scott's marriage breaking up. They were totally unsuited, of course— Janis is utterly selfish and unscrupulous.' She had shrugged. 'But love is blind. I only hope Scott isn't going to bury himself in the Grampians forever as a result. He could have a wonderful career ahead of him in one of our big hospitals if he doesn't leave it too late.' She had eyed Anna sharply. 'I suppose you won't be thinking of marriage until you've qualified?' It had sounded like an injunction.

Anna had answered no, and had received approving looks from both the Carters.

Scott said now, 'Have you heard anything about your application?'

Anna shook her head. 'Not yet. Professor Carter told me it would take time.'

'Don't worry,' he assured her, 'he'll see you get a place.'

Anna said guiltily, 'I feel I might be jumping the queue, his pulling strings for me. . .'

'Don't be ridiculous. John Carter wouldn't pull strings for anyone he didn't believe would be worthwhile.'

'But he doesn't know much about me.'

'My dear girl, he found out all he needed to know in an hour's conversation. He's a genius at summing people up. And besides, your qualifications are excellent.'

Anna wondered if the surgeon's wife was also good at summing people up, and if her comment on Scott's wife was accurate. She longed to ask Scott what was happening, whether he was still considering a reconciliation with Janis, but felt it would be prying to do so. He would tell her if he wanted to, and at the moment he evidently preferred not to talk about it.

She felt in her bones that he was probably moving towards giving their marriage another go. Scott was the kind of man who didn't give up easily, and if he had been blaming himself for the break-up of the marriage, which she sensed he would have been, then he would not be able to refuse the chance to make amends. But since the blame was unlikely to have been all his, however hard he tried, the marriage could fall apart again. And the second failure, Anna thought, would be devastating.

'Your friend Meg's wedding is this Saturday, isn't it?' Scott said.

'Yes. You know Peter Robbins, of course. He's Mrs Silver's GP.'

'Mmm. She'll be in good hands, I think.' He smiled. 'I mean Meg *and* Mrs Silver! Peter's a conscientious young fellow. You're bridesmaid?'

Anna nodded. 'You're coming?' She knew Meg had invited him.

'I don't know at this stage. I might have to go to Melbourne.'

To see Janis, she thought. There had been no talk of bushwalking lately and Scott had not been on the two occasions she had gone herself. She guessed he was spending as much time with his wife as he could. It looked as though they were making a serious attempt to talk things over and patch up their differences.

He chatted on about nothing much, and all at once it occurred to Anna that he was making conversation for the sake of it, lingering in her office for some reason.

Finally he said, 'There's a good bushwalk this Sunday, a fairly tough one, Would you feel up to tackling it after the wedding?'

'I was aiming to go,' Anna said, 'but I thought you said you might be going to Melbourne.'

'I'm not planning to stay over.'

She was curious, but Scott did not enlarge on his plans. 'Well, if you're going,' she said. 'It's a bit far for me to cycle, so I'd need a lift.'

'You just got offered one.'

'Thanks.'

Their words dissolved into silence, and Scott's grey eyes held Anna's with the unfathomable look she had lately become accustomed to. Since any kind of look from those eyes melted her bone marrow, she wrenched her gaze away and pretended to look urgently for something on her desk, wishing he'd go, yet wanting him to stay, and as a result feeling her emotional equilibrium in grave danger of toppling.

It was a relief when his pager emitted its electronic summons. She was not so relieved to find that there was an emergency, which meant another bed to be found in an already full ward.

'What we can do,' she said to Fran a few minutes later, 'is cram another bed into Room Three for the time being. Linda Walker's due to be discharged tomorrow. . .' She paused, tapping her bottom lip thoughtfully. 'I wonder if she'd like to go home tonight.

I'll ask Scott. I'm sure her husband would be able to pick her up. He'll probably be coming in to visit her anyway this evening, and she can't wait to get out of here.'

Fran agreed. 'She's in the day-room now, so we could remake her bed right away and then we wouldn't have to search for a spare one.'

Anna went along to the day-room, where ambulant patients were watching television or reading. Linda Walker, a young woman of nineteen or twenty and noticeably pregnant, was knitting a small white garment. She looked up as Anna approached her chair. The large gauze patch over her left eye was the outward evidence of an eye injury, sustained when she had tripped and fallen, breaking a bottle. A piece of glass had stabbed her eye, and she had come within a hair's breadth of losing her sight. There had also been some anxiety about the baby, but fortunately no harm had come to it when Linda had fallen.

'Hello, Sister,' Linda greeted Anna, and heaved a pleased sigh. 'I'm allowed home tomorrow, I believe.'

'That's what Dr Carroll said this morning,' agreed Anna. 'So long as you come to Outpatients as often as he asks you to. It won't be for very long—your eye is healing up very nicely. How does it feel?'

'Fine. It's not painful at all now, and, as you know, when Dr Carroll took the dressing off this morning I could see quite well.' Linda looked bleak for an instant. 'I was so scared! What if I was blind in that eye? I don't think I could have borne it.'

'Well, you're not, thanks to some adroit surgical skill.'

'I know. And you've all looked after me wonderfully,' Linda said. 'I shan't be a bit nervous when I come in to have my baby. I know the ropes now.'

'Don't count on it yet,' said Anna, 'but I might be able to let you go home tonight, if you want to, and Dr Carroll agrees. There's an emergency in Theatre right now and we're short of a bed.' She laughed. 'You're the only one we can spare! But I just wanted to check, before I ask Dr Carroll, that your husband would be able to fetch you.'

Linda's face lit up. 'He'd better be!' She giggled. 'I bet there'll be a sink full of dishes, and a laundry full of filthy overalls all of which he intends to wash tonight. But never mind. . .anything's worth it to go home.'

Anna nodded sympathetically. 'You've been missing him.'

'And how! I just hope he's been missing me as much. Gee, I never thought I'd feel that way. I mean, being in love and getting married and all that is a big hype, isn't it? But then you settle down and life's ordinary again—except for being pregnant, of course—and you don't realise how quickly you can take having someone there all the time for granted.'

'I suppose it must be like that,' Anna agreed.

Linda folded her knitting in her lap. 'You're not married, Sister?'

'No.'

Linda grinned. 'Well, you're wise not to rush into it, but if you happen to meet the right one before you're ready what do you do—ask him to hang around while you grow up?' She laughed ruefully. 'I didn't want to get married till I was twenty-five at least, but there was no way I was going to ask Warren to hang around for more than a week and have him snapped up by someone else! They don't come any better than my Warren.'

Oh, yes, they do, thought Anna. Scott Carroll, for instance. But that was only her opinion. Everyone had their own private hero. Would she ever meet a man to match him? she wondered. Perhaps she would never get married. Anna sighed as she went to find Fran and organise the smooth reception of the new patient. The possibility was a long time ahead, anyway. For the next six years, if she was accepted at medical school, she was going to concentrate on her studies and nothing else. And maybe once she was qualified she would find so much fulfilment in her work that she would not want to marry at all.

'You look as though you're having gloomy thoughts,' remarked Fran, noticing Anna's deep frown.

Anna shook herself. 'No, not really. I was just contemplating the long years of study ahead.' She had told Fran of her plans recently.

'You're not getting cold feet, I hope.'

'No. From wondering if I really wanted to do it, I'm now just afraid I won't get a place next year. I don't think I could wait another year. It's now or never.'

'Well, keep thinking positive,' advised Fran, heading for the linen cupboard. 'Remember no news is good news.'

A short time later the emergency patient arrived in the ward. She was Denise Lavery, a teenager who had fractured her clavicle when she'd fallen while playing tennis. With an over-anxious mother hovering, she was installed in Linda's remade bed, and then Anna spent some time reassuring Mrs Lavery that Denise's injury was quite common, not serious, and that the bone would knit in about three weeks.

'She won't have to stay in hospital long,' Anna told the girl's mother. 'But she'll need the neck brace for a while.'

Anna was almost ready to go off duty and Scott had not yet appeared in the ward as he usually did to check on any patients he had operated on. There must have been some other urgent demand on his attention, she realised. And she hadn't asked him whether Linda could go home tonight instead of tomorrow.

It was with great relief that she finally saw him coming along the corridor, just as she was about to have him paged. He was looking tired, she thought again, as though he wasn't sleeping well. Janis's fault? Anna supposed it must be.

'I was just going to have you paged,' she told him.

'Something important?' He followed her back into her office.

'Yes and no.' She explained the situation briefly. Scott nodded, and Anna felt relieved all over again. It would not have been a surprise if he'd taken her to task for pre-empting his decision.

'Yes, I see no reason why not,' he said. 'Providing her husband's able to fetch her.'

'Oh, I'm sure he will be. I think they've been missing each other.'

Scott looked steadily into her face. 'Well, which do you want first, the good news or the bad?'

Anna tensed. 'Scott, what do you mean?'

He clasped her shoulder in a firm grip. 'You're in.'

'I'm in. . .?'

'Melbourne Uni Med School next year. John Carter rang me and said there should be a letter in your mail today. He sent congratulations and wished you luck.'

Anna felt weak. 'I can't believe it!'

Scott was smiling, but there was a strange wistful look in his eyes that she did not understand. 'You will when you pick up your mail.'

She wanted to throw her arms around him with gratitude, but she resisted the temptation and said, 'Thank you for all you've done, Scott. I really am very grateful.'

'You deserve a break,' he said softly.

Anna was beginning to feel elated, and it was like champagne bubbles fizzing through her veins. She could hardly wait to collect the mail from the post office box on her way home. At last, after all this time, she was going to start studying medicine again.

'So what's the bad news?' she asked.

He laughed. 'That was the bad news!' He reached out and lightly smoothed the lines between her eyebrows. 'The good news is that they've accepted you for second-year entry.'

She could hardly believe it. 'Are you sure?'

Scott cupped her face in his hands and lightly kissed her. 'Positive. Congratulations.'

'I feel weak at the knees,' Anna said shakily.

'I must be improving!'

'Not you! Because I really didn't expect. . .' She leaned against the desk for support. 'Oh, Scott, it's such wonderful news!'

'You won't get cold feet now?'

She shook her head. 'No. Now it's really happened I can't wait to get started.' Her face was already flushed with excitement. 'After all these years. . .at last. . .' She covered her face with her hands, speechless.

Scott prised her fingers away, and with humour in his eyes said, 'Now the really bad news.'

'What. . .?' Anna's elation became alarm.

'You'll be getting three new admissions tomorrow.'

She groaned. 'But we're full up!'

'This is a hospital, not a hotel,' Scott said with mock severity. 'I'll see what can be done about discharging a couple more besides Linda,' he promised. 'You can probably cram another bed in somewhere.'

She pulled a face. 'That's what you doctors always say. What are they?'

He considered. 'The cholycystectomy could probably wait a week, although the patient is suffering quite a bit of discomfort, but I'm anxious to do the cystoscopy pretty urgently because I'm a bit suspicious about what I might find, likewise the D & C.'

Anna voiced a perennial complaint. 'We ought to have a separate gynae ward.'

'I know. I've mentioned it myself, so has the local gynaecologist, but it seems the Board can't see the necessity.'

She sighed resignedly. 'I don't know why we don't go in for double bunks, and fork-lifts to shift the patients!'

Scott laughed. 'What a brilliant notion!' Suddenly he threw his arm around her shoulder and held her against him. 'I love your wry way of looking at things, Anna. I suppose it's your British sense of humour.'

Anna coloured furiously, wishing that close contact with Dr Carroll did not bring on symptoms she would prefer not to experience. He let her go quickly, as though startled too. There was still a strong physical awareness between them, she realised, and knew that he was shaken by it too.

'I was trained in the stiff upper lip school, if that's what you mean,' she said with a grin.

'You were born with a philosophical outlook on life,'

Scott declared, 'and experience has honed it. You have the patience and fortitude to be a doctor,' he added, smiling at her. 'Rather more than I have!'

'You seem to be making out all right,' said Anna. 'Professor Carter and his wife think very highly of you, by the way.'

He grimaced modestly. 'Do they? That's good for the flagging ego.' The look he gave her was enigmatic and she wondered if there was any significance in the remark. Was Janis an ego-blaster, even when wanting a reconciliation?

Her curiosity could not be contained any longer, and she asked, 'How's Janis?'

Scott's eyes narrowed and darkened, and his face muscles tensed. 'What you mean is, have I made up my mind yet? The answer is no, Anna, I haven't.'

'You've been seeing her a lot lately, I suppose?'

'Once or twice.'

Now that she'd been brave enough to open the subject and Scott had not rebuffed her, perversely Anna suddenly did not want to know the intimate details of his attempt at mending his marriage.

He went on, 'Mostly I've been going off on my own trying to think the whole thing through.'

'The moment will come when you know,' she said with conviction. 'It'll all come together and you'll find you've made your decision without realising it.'

He lifted his hand and idly smoothed the glossy brown strands that swept back from her forehead to the chignon at the back of her head. 'You've made it harder for me. . .'

'Me?' Anna felt her heart skip a beat.

His fingertips traced the shape of her ear and slid around to her nape. 'Yes. . .' His voice was very soft, the grey eyes very compelling. 'There's the what-might-have-been factor to be considered.'

Anna, horrified at the swift heating of her blood, backed away. 'Now you're talking in riddles.'

Scott lowered his hand reluctantly. 'Yes, I am—rambling like an idiot. Take no notice, Anna. I'm not myself lately.'

You haven't been yourself for quite some time, she thought with concern. 'I hope it all works out all right soon,' she said.

He grinned. 'As I said, you're much more patient than I am, much more resigned to letting life take its course.'

Anna thought she couldn't bear to have him there much longer. He was getting to her in a very disturbing way. 'I'd appreciate it if you'd put your mind to deciding who can go home tomorrow,' she said in a return to a brisk tone.

Scott took the hint and went off to examine the patients whom he thought were candidates for early discharge. Anna knew he would not allow anyone to go home if there was the slightest chance of their having any problems.

Saturday was a fine mild day, with a slight breeze and a few fluffy clouds scudding across the sky.

'Perfect for a wedding,' declared Anna, the first to venture outside that morning to test the temperature. 'Happy is the bride the sun shines on.'

'Nervous is the bride. . .' muttered Meg through chattering teeth as she chewed a piece of toast as though it were cardboard.

Anna laughed. 'Why? You're in love, all your friends are coming to see you marry Peter, and the future looks rosy. There's no need to look as though you're going to an execution!'

Meg scowled. 'You wait till it's your turn. You'll be nervous too.'

'Oh, come on,' urged Anna. 'Everything's under control. Your parents have arrived on time, your dress is superb and the flowers will be here any minute. So, if I'm not mistaken, will your mother and father, so don't you think you ought to get a move on? Time flies when you're getting ready for a special occasion, and you mustn't be *too* late.'

Meg swallowed a mouthful of orange juice and seemed slightly cheered. 'No, you're right, I'd better get moving.'

Meg's parents, who were staying in a local motel, arrived soon after breakfast, and the time did fly. But after a few minor panics it all went off without a hitch. The wedding was at midday, in the Memorial Gardens in Mount William, a spot favoured for outdoor weddings. Meg wore a cream silk dress and loose jacket with a matching picture hat, and carried orchids. Anna's dress was in palest chartreuse, with an orchid corsage. Peter in a light fawn suit was handsome and more nervous than Meg, but their tentative smiles as they came together before the marriage celebrant soon relaxed into laughter as the ceremony ended.

Anna watched with envy their happiness explode into little intimacies, a touch, a squeeze, a kiss, and the kind of eye contact that meant the exchange of lovers' secrets. Foolishly she kept thinking of Scott, and was glad he was not there because that would have made it all the more poignant. It did not help, however, to think of him with Janis, to imagine their rediscovery of the kind of sweetness Meg and Peter were enjoying.

She almost wished she hadn't agreed to go bushwalking the next day. Being with Scott was painful now, and she would be on tenterhooks because one of these days—tomorrow even—he would suddenly tell her that he and Janis were getting back together again. If they did, he would probably arrange to leave Mount William before the year was up. No doubt another doctor could be found to fill the post until Russ Phillips came back. If that happened it would make life easier for her, Anna thought, until she too left. Would she ever run into Scott in Melbourne? she wondered. Or Janis? It was likely, she supposed. She must make sure that if she did neither must ever guess her true feelings for Scott.

Her thoughts rambled on aimlessly during the reception at the Mount William Hotel, and she was still only half in the present by the time Meg and Peter left for their honeymoon. Meg threw her bouquet of orchids into Anna's hands, and everyone laughed and said she would be next. But they always said that at weddings, and it was pure superstition that bridesmaids who caught bouquets were next to be married. One could hardly avoid catching the bouquet, Anna thought bemusedly.

On Sunday morning, Anna woke with a heavy head. She supposed she must have drunk too much champagne at the wedding, and later when she had joined Meg's parents for dinner.

Remembering she was supposed to be going bushwalking, she staggered out of bed and showered, then made some coffee and toast. The headache subsided a little after persuasion from a couple of paracetamols. She could pretend it hadn't and cry off, she thought. . . But she didn't have the will power to do that.

Scott was prompt as always. 'How was the wedding?' he asked cheerfully. In fact he looked more relaxed than Anna had seen him for quite a while.

'Great. The bride looked beautiful, the groom was very handsome, and it all went off without a hitch.'

'And what about the bridesmaid?' His eyes were teasing.

'She didn't fall flat on her face or spill wine down her expensive dress! She had dinner with Meg's parents and fell into bed thinking weddings were rather more tiring than ward duties.'

Scott laughed softly. 'A good brisk walk will liven you up. It's a beautiful day again.'

Anna agreed. She loaded the lunch into their backpacks and joined Scott in the car. She wanted to ask how was Melbourne, but didn't. She gazed out of the window waiting for him to start the conversation again, but he drove in silence. It was a good fifteen minutes before it occurred to Anna that they were not going in the direction of the meeting point for that day's walk.

'Scott. . .' she said tentatively. 'I hate to say this, but you're going the wrong way.'

He slowed briefly to let a magpie cross the road, then glanced at her. 'No, I'm not.'

She felt bound to insist, 'This isn't the road to Hall's Gap, unless we're going a very long way round, and there isn't time. . .'

'I know. We're not going to Hall's Gap. The venue has been changed.'

Anna was puzzled. No one had told her. But of course she'd been at the wedding yesterday and out last night if someone had tried to contact her. It was very unusual for venues to be changed at short notice. It had never happened before.

'Where are we going?' she asked.

'Singleton Falls.'

She drew in a sharp breath. 'We went there a few weeks ago. . .' That was where Scott had first kissed her.

'And that's where we're going today,' said Scott.

A tiny suspicion began to grow in her mind. 'Who contacted you to say the venue was changed?'

He looked straight ahead. 'No one. I rang Brent Wilson and told him we wouldn't be coming today.'

Anna swivelled as far as her seatbelt would allow. 'Scott, what is this? Why did you do that?'

He answered softly without looking at her. 'Because I want to go bushwalking with you without all those others around. I want to talk to you.' He swung round a bend and a long straight stretch of road lay ahead. When he turned to look at her briefly, his eyes were sombre. 'I wanted us to be alone,' he said.

CHAPTER TEN

ANNA knew without asking what Scott wanted to talk to her about. Janis. He was going to tell her what he had decided. She was sure she already knew what that was. He was going to try and make a go of his marriage. It was inevitable, of course, that he would, Anna thought. He had merely been waiting around hoping that Janis would make a move, and she had. There really hadn't been a decision to make, but for the sake of his pride Scott would have had to pretend that there was. Reconciliation was what he wanted.

She was flattered that he wanted to tell her, although not sure she really wanted to hear what he had to say. But there was no way she could get out of it without sounding uncaring or, worse, revealing her true feelings for him. If Scott wanted moral support for his decision, she would give it to him, even though she had misgivings about the rightness of what he intended to do. Feeling noble about it, she thought wryly, was one way to cover the pain. There had never been the slightest chance for her with Scott, and she was a fool to have let her emotions run away with her. Even if he weren't going back to Janis, he would never risk marrying another career woman, and especially another doctor. He'd made that perfectly clear.

'It's a great day for a hike,' he commented as they hoisted their backpacks over their shoulders and set off from the picnic area.

'Fabulous,' Anna agreed, sweeping her gaze across the clear sky. 'Perfect temperature.'

They walked steadily for some time without speaking, and she wondered uneasily when Scot would tell her of his decision. When he did break the silence it was only to point out birds and help her to make a sighting. With their heads together over the field guide identifying what they saw, there was a certain intimacy which frayed her nerve-ends raw.

Mid-morning they paused for coffee, and as she shrugged out of her backpack and sat down on a convenient log Anna thought, This is it. Now he'll tell me.

But Scott talked only about birds. It almost seemed that he was deliberately avoiding the subject of his marriage. Once or twice their eyes met and his expression made Anna's pulse race expectantly, but then he would take on that withdrawn look again and still said nothing. She began to get jittery. As soon as she had finished her mug of coffee, she stowed her Thermos back in her backpack and stood up.

'Ready?' At least when they were walking she didn't feel quite so uneasy.

Scott nodded and they set off again. After a few minutes, he said suddenly, 'How do you feel now you're assured of a place in med school next year?'

'Scared! Especially as I'll be starting in second year. I keep thinking someone must have made a mistake and I'll get a letter any day telling me so.'

He laughed. 'You must feel elated too?'

'Yes, of course—I'm overwhelmed. It's what I always wanted, Scott, and I can hardly believe it's going to come true at last. I just hope I'll be able to cope, being a late starter.'

'You'll cope,' he said confidently. 'I don't think you'll let yourself be distracted.'

Anna said firmly, 'I intend to work hard. I know it won't be easy, but it'll be worth it.'

Silence descended again except for the occasional pause to birdwatch, and around midday they arrived at the waterfall. The curtain of water fell noisily from a fissure high up in the cliff face, and the cloud of fine spray hovered over the bush below as before, moved gently by the slight breeze until it evaporated in the filtered sunshine. For a moment Anna stood still, wrapped in the memory of the last time she had been there.

'We'd better sit over there,' Scott was pointing, 'if we don't want to get damp.'

They scrambled over rocks and rivulets to reach an outcrop of sunwarmed sandstone where acacias were flowering and the purple pea flowers of the hardenbergias were intertwined with the undergrowth. A grey butcher bird gave a fluting call as it flew from the gum tree near where they intended to picnic into a tree a little further away.

'He's not going too far,' Anna observed. 'He knows picnickers when he sees them.' She slipped her backpack off her shoulders and chose a spot where there was another rock for a backrest.

Scott sprawled close beside her. 'Peaceful. . .' he murmured, looking at the sky. Then he looked at her and smiled in the sultry, enigmatic way he sometimes did which sent feathery tingles down her spine.

Anna wondered how much longer she could contain her impatience. Why didn't Scott get it over with? All he had to say was, 'I'm going back to Janis. I wanted to let you know, as you've been so understanding.'

Inwardly, she laughed at herself. Why should she expect him to pay her a compliment? She'd commiserated with him once or twice, that was all.

Their sandwiches and fruit were soon eaten, and the rest of the coffee consumed. Anna lay back against the warm rock watching a rainbow which had appeared in the spray from the waterfall. If there were a pot of gold at the foot of that rainbow, she mused fancifully, you'd need a pneumatic drill to get at it through the rock. The shimmering rainbow and the sound of falling water were hypnotic and she almost fell asleep. Scott's voice, however, suddenly penetrated.

'Anna. . .'

She turned her head and held her breath. 'Yes?'

'I thought you might be interested to know that I saw Janis on Saturday. We had a long discussion.'

Anna felt a dark wave rolling over her, drowning her, but she forced herself to listen. 'I guessed you were with her. I'm not surprised, Scott. I always thought you'd end up going back to her, and I hope you'll be happier this time. . .' The words came out in a rush as though she'd rehearsed them.

There was a fleeting sadness in his eyes, but also firm resolve. 'I'm not going back to her, Anna.'

Shock and disbelief were Anna's instant reactions, but Scott's face told her that he meant what he had said.

'But I thought. . .' She was stunned, but she dared to ask, 'Why not?'

He was forthright. 'It wouldn't work, Anna, because it would be for the wrong reasons. We should never have married in the first place. And I know she only wants me back now because the American job fell through and she needs to have her morale boosted. If

I went back to her she'd pretend to all her friends that she'd turned down the US job because "Scott begged and pleaded with me to go back to him".' His mouth twisted. 'She'd play at being a martyr for a while, and when that novelty wore off. . .' He shrugged. 'In any case, if I went back to Janis it would only be out of pride, because I was still refusing to admit I'd made a mistake, that I was a failure. That's no basis for a reconciliation.'

'I'm glad you realised that,' Anna said quietly.

Their eyes met, and the power of their attraction for each other had never been greater. Anna's heart was flipping erratically enough to put a cardiologist in a panic.

Scott reached across the space between them and stroked her hand where it lay on the rock. She withdrew it abruptly.

'Anna. . .' His voice was husky, his eyes betraying his emotion. Anna knew that hers would be a giveaway too. 'Do you know,' he said softly, 'some of the best times of my life have been spent with you? You're always just yourself, never role-playing, or seeking personal advantage. You're so natural and nice.' He smiled sensuously. 'It drives me crazy wanting to make love to you, but I'm never more content than when I'm with you.'

Anna wondered how she was supposed to interpret such words. 'It's my training,' she joked. 'I got ten out of ten for bedside manner!'

'I'll teach you to mock!' Taking her by surprise, he pulled her towards him and rolled over on to his back so that she found herself spreadeagled across his body. They were both laughing, but the laughter quickly died as the strength of another more primal emotion submerged them. His face was close, and his lips were reaching for hers. Anna closed her eyes as the sensual warmth of his mouth brushed hers lightly, then crushed it with an urgent hunger. A wave of need engulfed her, and she felt its parallel shudder through him as he pressed her hard against his taut muscular thighs and trapped her legs between his own.

When he drew his lips away from hers for a moment, her eyes flipped open and read stark desire in his. 'Anna. . .' There was anguish in the way he whispered her name. 'Oh, Anna, I want you so much. . .'

Anna's strength of will was weakening. She could resist a mere sexual attraction, but love complicated life. Unless he loved her. . . 'Scott. . .' Her voice was a faint protest in the back of her throat, hardly audible.

He gave her no chance to say more. It was as though the tight rein he'd kept on himself was suddenly slackened, and he gathered her into an embrace that almost cracked her ribs and robbed her of breath. It did more than that. It robbed her of reason temporarily, and she gave herself up to the fires that were burning so fiercely inside her, and without doubt in him too. The sound of the waterfall pounding into the pool seemed to fill her head with sound, to blot out the world and leave her stranded in a space bubble with the man she loved so much it hurt. She could not think, and had no choice but to surrender her will to his and take the consequences.

In the heat of passion they had forgotten where they were. It was Anna who suddenly became aware and gasped, 'Scott, no, not here. . .someone might come. . .'

He looked dazed, then groaned. 'Damn!' He rolled over on to his stomach, and she ran her fingers through his tousled hair, picking out the bits of grass and seed that had clung to it.

'Sorry. . .' He sat up and grasped her fiercely. 'Anna. . . Anna. . .' He pushed aside her unbuttoned shirt and buried his head against her warm rounded breasts once more. 'I wish. . .Oh, God, you're so beautiful. . .so special. . .' And then abruptly he reinstated control. A shaky laugh burst out of him as he traced her jawline with a tender finger. 'We'd be so good together, Anna.'

Anna had regained her common sense. 'I don't think that would be wise.'

He grinned at her suddenly. 'Do you always have to be wise? Why not be frivolous for once? You don't want to get involved, neither do I. We'd be protection for each other.'

She gave a brief laugh. 'Do you know what you're suggesting?'

Scott's face was grave, but his eyes were still smouldering. 'Anna, I'm not suggesting marriage,' he said, as though she were scorning it. 'We have our own ways to go, you to become a doctor and I—well, I'd be a fool to risk getting involved in the same kind of nightmare again, wouldn't I? But what could be wrong with us getting together now and then. . .?'

His words doused the faint hope Anna had foolishly allowed to flare. 'For a little sexual relief, you mean?' she said harshly. 'A jolly little now-and-then affair?'

Scott looked hurt. 'You're making it sound sordid!'

'It is sordid,' she said. 'We'd be making use of each other in the worst possible way.'

He tried smiling to soften her angry look. 'I thought it would be in the nicest possible way.'

She was really angry with him now. 'That's typical of

a man! Utterly insensitive. So long as your needs are satisfied, you don't give a damn about anyone else, do you?'

He grasped her hand and held it tightly, although she tried to wrench it away. 'Anna, that's not fair. . .You have needs too, and you can't deny it. You were as aroused as I was a moment ago. We could have a lot of fun together, and not just in bed—I like you a lot, I admire you, and we seem to have a lot in common. What's wrong with a relationship that has no strings attached?' He paused. 'You'll get horribly lonely if you keep yourself to yourself for the next five years, especially as you're not the kind of woman to toss lovers on and off like sweaters.'

Anna could not tell him why a relationship with no strings attached was impossible, that a one-sided love was worse than no love at all. She stood up and walked down to the edge of the pool below the waterfall, her emotions in turmoil, too choked to speak.

Scott followed and slid his arms around her waist and rested his cheek against her hair. 'What's the matter?'

Anna turned on him furiously, her control snapping. 'You great clod, can't you see? Can't you *see*. . .?' She wrenched free of him, and faced him with blazing eyes. Anger was her only defence against the mounting misery inside her. Then with an effort of will she summoned a temporary indifference and said, 'It's OK, don't take any notice of me, Scott. I'm a bit. . .well. . .' Her words evaporated, and her head seemed to be spinning out of control again.

He approached her, a puzzled expression in his grey eyes. 'Anna, I've never seen you so uptight. . .' As she stared at him like a cornered animal, the light of realisation began to dawn in his eyes. He caught hold of her hands. 'Anna, don't. . .don't fall in love with me. Is that why you. . .?' He grasped her shaking shoulders. 'Anna—oh, God, this is terrible! I'm sorry—I wasn't looking for. . . Hell, I've been a blind fool, haven't I?'

'You don't have to apologise,' she said, gathering the shreds of her dignity together. 'You don't have to do anything, Scott. . .' Her fragile control collapsed again, and suddenly there was only one way out of the awful humiliating predicament she was in, and that was to run. 'Just leave me alone!' she sobbed, and like a wounded animal that saw a last chance of escape, she turned and ran blindly into the bush.

She heard Scott call out, but she did not look back. She wanted to get as far away from him as she could. Desperate misery welled up in her and spurred her on. She gave no thought to where she was going, just plunged on through the bush, slamming through the undergrowth, swerving instinctively to avoid trees, her mind a confusion of emotions. The noise she made crashing through the bush drowned out any calling from behind her, and when at last she was forced to stop by a stitch in her side, and leaned against a tree, her own rasping breath was the only sound in her ears.

Gradually her breathing subsided to a more normal rate, and with the calm that followed panic she looked around her. She was deep in unfamiliar territory. But not lost, she told herself firmly. She could easily find her way back. Scott was probably following her anyway. He'd catch up with her in a minute. She half smiled now as she thought of how she'd outstripped him, and then she remembered why she'd run, and a wave of chill despair washed over her. What an idiot he must think her! But she would have to face him and apologise. With dread, she started back. The sun had been behind her as she ran, so all she had to do was walk into it and call out occasionally.

She tried to call out, but her mouth was dry and only a pitiful squeak came out. She realised she was terribly thirsty, but there was no water where she was. She moistened her lips with a tongue that now felt thick and dry. Her legs were rubbery and she felt dizzy. But Scott couldn't be far behind. She tried to call again, but still the sound seemed to travel no further than the next tree. And he wasn't calling. If only he would call, she could make for the sound.

Keeping the lid tightly on her panic, she trudged wearily back through the bush, with the sun in her eyes. How was she going to face him? He would be angry with her, and disappointed. And she'd committed the unforgivable sin of revealing that she was in love with him. She had given him a new burden. She must relieve him of it somehow, she thought. She must convince him that her wild flight had some other basis or that she was just—just what? Her brain offered no plausible explanation.

'Oh, God, why did I make such a fool of myself?' she whimpered, dragging herself wearily through bushes that scratched and tangled and seemed put there deliberately as obstacles.

And then all at once she heard a faint 'Cooee!'

'Scott!' she squeaked. 'I'm here!' But there was no way he could have heard her. 'Just keep calling,' she prayed, and gave thanks as the sound penetrated the silence once more.

She staggered towards it, desperately trying to moisten her mouth enough to call in reply. Eventually she managed a creditable call, and to her joy it was answered. Gathering her last reserves of strength, she plunged on, until to her chagrin she suddenly came to a dead end. She was at the edge of a cliff and there was a steep drop of thirty or forty feet into the bush below. How had she got there? she wondered in amazement. And then from below came another loud call.

'Scott!' she yelled. 'Scott. . .' She saw him, coming through the trees towards the foot of the cliff. He was limping. Anna's brow creased anxiously. How had he injured himself? She felt guiltily that it was her fault. He looked up.

'Anna!'

'Oh, Scott. . .' she whimpered, tears sliding down her cheeks. 'I'm coming. . .' she said in a choked voice.

He called out urgently, 'Stay where you are. Don't move, or you'll get lost again. I'll be up with you in a minute.'

Anna stared at him as, despite whatever injury he had sustained, he backtracked and began to climb the steep incline some yards away from the vertical part of the cliff, where it provided the easiest ascent. She took a step to make her way towards the point where he would reach the top, and as she did so a considerable portion of the edge of the cliff gave way beneath her feet. Uttering a shrill scream of terror, she plunged downwards with a landslide of rocks, bushes torn out by the roots, and earth. She heard Scott give a strangled shout, earth filled her mouth and eyes and ears, something hit her with a dull thud on the back of the neck and she knew no more.

CHAPTER ELEVEN

'SHE's coming round! Get Dr Carroll!'

Anna, who had been semi-conscious for some time, heard the voice as from the other side of a curtain, a voice that was vaguely familiar, but she couldn't place who it was. She opened her eyes and this time they stayed open. Details began to register. She was lying on her side. The walls were white. She was in bed. There was someone else in the room, outside her line of vision, then within it, bending over her, smiling—a woman in a pale blue uniform. A nurse.

'Anna. . .' the nurse was saying softly. 'Hello! Come back to us at last, have you? Welcome! Dr Carroll will be relieved.'

'Anna?' Anna murmured the name in a puzzled tone, then said, 'Sorry—you're Anna.' Her wits were slow. What was she doing in bed, with a nurse. . .? God, hospital! She was in hospital. Hurt. How. . .?

As panic gripped her, she tried to sit up. 'What's wrong with me? What happened?' She clasped her head trying to remember, but there was a terrible void, a total blank. And her hands made contact with a bandage. Oh, God, she'd injured her head. She took her hands away slowly. Something was pulling at the inside of her elbow. She stared at the tube attached to her arm as she fell back against the pillow.

The nurse placed that arm gently back on the counterpane and examined the patch where the tube entered Anna's arm. 'Careful, you'll pull the tube out, though I dare say Dr Carroll will want to remove it anyway now you're awake. It's all right, Anna, you're not badly hurt. Lie back, and don't upset yourself.' She propped another pillow behind Anna's head. 'It looks as though you've temporarily lost your memory, but don't worry, it'll come back. It's just the concussion.' She beamed. 'I'm Fran. You don't remember me?'

Anna shook her head. 'No. . .' She asked tentatively, '*My* name's Anna?'

'Anna Mackay,' Fran told her. 'Sister in charge on the women's surgical ward at Mount William Hospital.' She searched Anna's face for some sign of recognition.

Anna was shaking her head, dismayed. 'I can't remember. . . What happened to me?'

Fran said gently, 'I think I'd better leave that for Dr Carroll to tell you. Scott Carroll—surely you remember him?' A smile briefly lightened her anxiety.

Anna shook her head.

'He'll be here in a minute. He said to call him the instant you recovered consciousness.' Fran smiled again. 'He's been a very worried man, Anna. He hardly left your bedside for days.'

Anna was startled. 'How long. . .have I been unconscious?'

'Nearly two weeks.'

'Two weeks!' Anna gasped. 'I've got brain damage!'

Fran laughed. 'I don't think so. Mind you, considering what happened, you were lucky not to injure your spine or fracture your skull. You were just shaken and bruised and rather heavily concussed, I'm afraid.'

'Where did it happen?' Vague images seemed to be trying to come together in Anna's mind, like clouds scudding across each other in a stormy sky, formless and insubstantial, impossible to grasp hold of.

Fran said firmly, 'Dr Carroll will explain.'

As she spoke the door opened and Anna found herself staring at a tall, brown-haired man with very handsome features, a little gaunt, but good-looking none the less. A faint warmth trickled along her veins, and as he approached the bed and looked down at her, grey eyes devouring her, she was gripped with the most astonishing sensation, and blushed. I know I should recognise him, she thought, distressed, but who *is* he? And why do I feel so. . .so *attracted* to him?

He sat on the bed and held her hand. 'Anna. . .at last!'

She heard Fran say quietly, 'She doesn't remember anything about the accident, Dr Carroll, or who she is and who we are.' She smiled again at Anna, reassuringly, and quietly went out.

Anna looked questioningly at the doctor. 'She said you would explain what happened. I can't remember anything. . .'

His dark eyebrows almost met in a deep frown. 'Nothing at all?'

Anna shook her head.

'You don't know me?' he asked.

'Only that you're a doctor,' she said. 'Please tell me what happened.'

There was deep pain in his eyes, which puzzled her. Then a dizzying thought struck her. There must be some personal connection between her and the doctor. She frowned, trying hard to remember. It was so frustrating.

Dr Carroll said, 'You were out bushwalking in the Grampians, last Sunday week. You were walking along the top of a cliff when part of it gave way, and you went down with a landslide and were almost buried by the rubble. A rock gave you one hell of a clout on the back of the head.'

'You were there?' Whether it was memory or intuition that made her think so was not clear to Anna.

He squeezed her hand tightly. 'I go bushwalking too. We belong to the same club.'

She felt a calming warmth. '*You* rescued me?'

'With a little help from the emergency services.'

'Fran said I'm not badly hurt.'

He shook his head. 'Thank God, no. You were covered in bruises and grazes, but by a miracle no bones were broken. You jarred your spine and gave your ankle a nasty twist, but that's all. Especially as you were practically buried alive. You slid most of the way down on top of the landslide as though you were tobogganning, until you reached the bottom and then the whole lot just broke up and buried you.'

'I was lucky there were other people there,' said Anna, shuddering.

The grey eyes met hers with a look she couldn't fathom. He said, 'Yes,' in an even more enigmatic tone.

'I feel so tired. . .' she whispered.

His fingers were on her pulse, and the touch was electrifying. Did she always react this way to doctors? she wondered.

'Go to sleep,' he said. 'You need a lot of rest. I'll come and see you again when you wake up, and we'll talk some more then. Maybe you'll start to remember.'

Anna's voice became slurred. 'I hope so. This is crazy, not even knowing my own name, or that nurse, or you, and yet I know I ought to. It's all there, muddled up.'

He rose, still holding her hand. 'You might never remember the actual accident,' he said, 'but you'll probably remember most of what happened prior to it.'

'I've got a strange feeling,' Anna murmured sleepily, 'that you're not just a doctor at the hospital where I work. . .'

To her surprise he bent and kissed her forehead. 'You're right there, Anna.'

Her eyelids were heavy. She had closed them before she heard the door close behind Dr Carroll. She strained to lift the veil that seemed to block her mind, but it stayed firmly in place. Except that she had a strange intuitive feeling that something was very wrong. As the thought took root, a terrible despair came with it and tears oozed out from under her closed lids and slid down her cheeks on to the pillow. There was something she knew instinctively she did not want to remember.

She slept for eight hours solid and woke with a start when a nurse came into her room.

'Hello, Fran,' she said, then clasped her hands over her ears. 'Fran—of course, it's you! How stupid of me—how could I have forgotten. . .?'

'It's all coming back, then?' Fran looked relieved. 'That's great. I thought we might have to wait a while longer.'

'Not everything.' Anna shook her head in frustration. 'I can't remember what happened—the accident—but I remember Meg's wedding, having dinner with her parents, going on a bushwalk. . .' She stopped short. Not an ordinary bushwalk, but alone with Scott. It was all coming back now, and a shudder ran through her as she recalled that day, what he had told her, and how she had reacted to him, then quarrelled with him and run off in a blind panic.

Fran checked her blood-pressure, pulse and temperature, then asked if she was hungry.

'Yes, I think I am,' muttered Anna.

'You were fed intravenously, of course, while you were unconscious,' said Fran, 'but I dare say you'd like some decent food!'

'Mmm. . .thanks.' Anna was trying to force her mind beyond that moment when she had run off into the bush, but there was just a brick wall.

'Dr Carroll will be along to see you shortly,' Fran said. 'I'll tell him you're awake.'

'No. . .' Anna caught a puzzled look from her. 'No, don't bother him.'

Fran smiled. 'He *wants* to be bothered, Anna!' She added, 'He's been nearly out of his mind with worry. He blames himself, of course, going off alone, just the two of you instead of with the usual group. It was pretty traumatic for him, I guess. Just as well he has a car phone, or it might have been ages longer before he could get help.' She smiled. 'You never let on you were going out with him, you dark horse! Well, from what I've seen this past fortnight, you couldn't have a better partner, and I reckon you're precisely what Doc Carroll needs.'

Anna shook her head. 'It isn't like that, Fran. . .'

But Fran wasn't listening. 'Simone and Liz send their love and they'll come and see you later when Dr Carroll says you can have visitors,' she said before hurrying away to inform Dr Carroll that his most precious patient was awake and seemed to have regained a good deal of her memory.

Anna lay and stared at the ceiling, but she had little time to mull it over, because within minutes he was in the room, smiling at her, sitting close and holding her hand.

'Hello, Anna.'

'Hello, Scott.'

'Fran tells me your memory's coming back.'

'Yes.' Anna looked at him with anguish. 'Scott, I'm so sorry. . . It was stupid of me running off like that.'

'You were upset.'

'That's no excuse. I shouldn't have gone over the top like that.'

He laughed. 'You sure did go over the top—literally!'

She managed a smile at her unintentional pun. 'I still can't remember that. It's coming back slowly. . . Now I remember stopping with a stitch, and thinking you must be right behind me, but you weren't, and I realised I was lost. It was a terrible feeling, but I tried to keep calm. I started walking back the way I was sure I'd come, then I heard you calling. I reached the edge of the cliff and saw you down below. . .' She stopped. 'You were limping.'

He answered the questions in her eyes. 'I would have caught up with you long before if I hadn't tripped and bashed my knee on a sharp rock. I thought for a minute I'd smashed the kneecap. By the time I started after you again, you were out of sight and I couldn't find you.'

'You still came after me, in spite of your knee,' Anna marvelled.

'I couldn't leave you. It was on the cards you'd get

lost. The bush is pretty dense around there, and in your emotional state anything could have happened.'

'Which it did,' she said slowly. Her brow creased in amazement. 'After I fell, you must have walked all the way back to the car to get help. That must have been agony!'

He squeezed her hand tightly. 'The only agony was not knowing how badly hurt you were. I made you as comfortable as I could on the spot because there was no way I could carry you to the car, and in case you recovered consciousness I left you a note.' He fumbled in his pocket and produced a crumpled sheet of folded paper torn from a notebook. He handed it to her. 'It says something I want you to know.'

Anna took the note and unfolded it. She read the pencilled words with incredulity.

Anna, have gone for help. Don't leave this spot—please! I'll be back soon. Don't try to run away again. I couldn't bear to lose you. I love you, and I want to marry you. Please believe I mean it. Scott.

'It was a good ruse to keep me stationary,' she said with a twisted little smile.

'It wasn't a ruse, it's true,' murmured Scott. He lifted her hand to his lips. 'I want to marry you—if you'll have me, of course!'

'You don't have to marry me because you feel guilty about—how I feel, and my nearly killing myself,' Anna told him. 'You needn't be afraid I'll do anything stupid again. It wasn't emotional blackmail.'

'I know it wasn't! Anna, please believe me. . . I do want to marry you.'

'But you vowed never to get involved again,' she said. 'You made it very clear that——'

'I know. That was how I felt—or thought I felt. I tried hard not to get involved with you, Anna. But I was involved, right from day one when I knocked you off your bike and thought I'd killed you. And then out there in the bush I thought I really had killed you. It was as though fate was trying hard to tell me something! When I dug you out of that rubble. . .'

'You dug me out?'

'With my bare hands. There was nothing else, and I didn't think I could do it, that you'd be asphyxiated before I uncovered you, but luckily you weren't too deeply buried and the earth was soft. I got some water from the creek and cleaned your face as best I could and washed your mouth, and all the time my fingers were straying to your pulse, fearfully. . . I knew then, Anna, that life wouldn't be worth living without you, that, in spite of myself, I loved you. I knew that you were one big reason I could never go back to Janis, that you were the woman I wanted to spend my life with, and I was a fool to be afraid it wouldn't work. You're not like Janis. You're sweet and funny and wonderful, and. . . I *love* you.'

'I thought you just wanted a now-and-then physical affair,' Anna said hesitantly, still not quite believing.

He sighed with deep remorse. 'I don't know how I could have been so cruel. I must have been blind not to know how you felt, not to realise that suggesting such a thing to you was an insult, but I was trying so hard not to fall in love with you—and I honestly thought you were concerned only with taking up medicine again, that you were a career woman. I was stupid enough to think that, like Janis, you only had a one-track mind.' He smiled ruefully. 'I even encouraged you, because subconsciously that's what I wanted you to be—a career woman—so I wouldn't risk falling in love with you. I didn't want to experience the pain of love ever again.'

'Oh, Scott. . .' Anna's eyes were bright with tears. 'It's all very well to say that, but truly I don't have to be a doctor. I don't want to do anything except be with you. . . If you're afraid it will make a difference, I won't do it. It's not important.'

He frowned at her and scolded, 'Don't lie! It's very important to you. You are going to be a doctor. You'll always hanker for that lost chance if you don't take it now. You made your sacrifice when you gave it up to look after your mother. You're not going to do that a second time. Not for me.'

'But you don't want a wife with a career—you said so.'

He bent forward and kissed her lips. 'I want *you* for my wife, Anna, and whatever you want I aim to help you achieve it.'

'But that's what led to conflict with Janis,' she protested.

Scott looked earnestly into her face and said with deep conviction, 'Because we weren't in love. You and I are different, Anna. You and I will work out the problems, not blame each other for them. We'll talk things over and compromise if we have to, because more important than either of our careers will be our need to be together.' He looked at her solemnly, anxiously. 'Say you agree with me.'

Anna felt the warmth of love filling her. 'I agree with you, Scott.'

Relief smoothed away his anxiety. 'Will you take a chance and marry me?'

She smiled. 'You're not free to marry yet.'

'In one month,' he told her, 'I will be.'

She murmured, 'Are you really sure you won't mind if I go to med school?'

'Of course I won't mind. I'll be immensely proud of you.' Scott smoothed a hair from her forehead. 'We might both have to make a few sacrifices, but we'll pull through. We have something special, Anna, that Janis and I never had. We're in love.'

Anna couldn't deny it. She dragged a hand across her eyes. 'Am I dreaming all this? Am I still unconscious? Delirious?'

He drew his fingers tenderly down her cheek. 'No, it's all real,' he said. 'Absolutely real.'

She reached her arms up and clasped her hands behind his neck. 'Oh, Scott, I do love you so much,' she whispered, laying her cheek against his. 'That's why I ran away. It hurt so much I couldn't bear it— that you didn't love me. . .'

'But I do, my darling,' he murmured against her ear. 'I was falling deeper and deeper in love with you all the time, only I wouldn't admit it. Haven't you noticed, men are somewhat stupider than women when it comes to their feelings? I had to nearly lose you to see just how precious you were to me, that nothing in the past was a reason for not letting myself love you.'

She sighed deeply. 'But I have to admit that I was "a stupid bloody wench"!'

Deep laughter rumbled through his ribcage. 'I think we'll reserve judgement on that.'

Anna pressed her lips to his. 'When can I be discharged? I feel fine now. Just a bit weak.'

'We need to keep an eye on you,' said Scott. A wicked glint came into his eye. 'What if I took you into my personal care? I think in that case I could safely discharge you quite soon—like tomorrow, maybe. . .'

She clasped his hand and lifted it to her lips, lightly kissing the palm. 'You couldn't make it tonight, could you?' she murmured silkily.

Scott smiled. 'I guess I could wangle it, Sister!'

AN EXCITING NEW SERIAL BY ONE OF THE WORLD'S BESTSELLING WRITERS OF ROMANCE

BARBARY WHARF is an exciting 6 book mini-series set in the glamorous world of international journalism.

Powerful media tycoon Nick Caspian wants to take control of the Sentinel, an old and well established British newspaper group, but opposing him is equally determined Gina Tyrell, whose loyalty to the Sentinel and all it stands for is absolute.

The drama, passion and heartache that passes between Nick and Gina continues throughout the series - and in addition to this, each novel features a separate romance for you to enjoy.

Read all about Hazel and Piet's dramatic love affair in the first part of this exciting new serial.

BESIEGED

Available soon

Price: £2.99

Discover the thrill of 4 Exciting Medical Romances – FREE

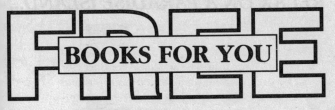

BOOKS FOR YOU

In the exciting world of modern
medicine, the emotions of true love
have an added drama. Now you can
experience four of these
unforgettable romantic tales of passion
and heartbreak FREE – and look forward to
a regular supply of Mills & Boon
Medical Romances delivered direct to your door!

🙠 🙠 🙠

Turn the page for details of 2 extra
free gifts, and how to apply.

An Irresistible Offer from Mills & Boon

Here's an offer from Mills & Boon to become a regular reader of Medical Romances. To welcome you, we'd like you to have four books, a cuddly teddy and a special MYSTERY GIFT, all absolutely free and without obligation.

Then, every month you could look forward to receiving 4 more **brand new** Medical Romances for £1.60 each, delivered direct to your door, post and packing free. Plus our newsletter featuring author news, competitions, special offers, and lots more.

This invitation comes with no strings attached. You can cancel or suspend your subscription at any time, and still keep your free books and gifts.

Its so easy. Send no money now. Simply fill in the coupon below and post it at once to -

Mills & Boon Reader Service, FREEPOST, PO Box 236, Croydon, Surrey CR9 9EL

NO STAMP REQUIRED

✂ - - - - - - - - - - - - - - - - - - -

YES! Please rush me my 4 Free Medical Romances and 2 Free Gifts! Please also reserve me a Reader Service Subscription. If I decide to subscribe, I can look forward to receiving 4 brand new Medical Romances every month for just £6.40, delivered direct to my door. Post and packing is free, and there's a free Mills & Boon Newsletter. If I choose not to subscribe I shall write to you within 10 days - I can keep the books and gifts whatever I decide. I can cancel or suspend my subscription at any time. I am over 18.

EP20D

Name (Mr/Mrs/Ms) _____

Address _____

_____

_____ Postcode _____

Signature _____

mps MAILING PREFERENCE SERVICE